Thomas Malory

King Arthur's Last Battle

PENGUIN EPICS

PENGUIN BOOKS

Published by the Penguin Group
Penguin Books Ltd, 80 Strand, London WC2R ORL, England
Penguin Group (USA) Inc., 375 Hudson Street, New York, New York 10014, USA
Penguin Group (Canada), 90 Eglinton Avenue East, Suite 700, Toronto, Ontario, Canada M4P 2Y3
(a division of Pearson Penguin Canada Inc.)
Penguin Ireland, 25 St Stephen's Green, Dublin 2, Ireland (a division of Penguin Books Ltd)
Penguin Group (Australia), 250 Camberwell Road, Camberwell, Victoria 3124, Australia
(a division of Pearson Australia Group Pty Ltd)
Penguin Books India Pvt Ltd, 11 Community Centre, Panchsheel Park, New Delhi – 110 017, India
Penguin Group (NZ), cnr Airborne and Rosedale Roads, Albany,
Auckland 1310, New Zealand (a division of Pearson New Zealand Ltd)
Penguin Books (South Africa) (Pty) Ltd, 24 Sturdee Avenue,
Rosebank, Johannesburg 2196, South Africa

Penguin Books Ltd, Registered Offices: 80 Strand, London WC2R ORL, England

www.penguin.com

L'Morte D'Arthur Volume I first published in Penguin Classics 1969
L'Morte D'Arthur Volume II first published in Penguin Classics 1969
These extracts published in Penguin Books 2006

I

All rights reserved

Taken from the Penguin Classics editions of L'Morte D'Arthur volumes I and II

Typeset by Rowland Phototypesetting Ltd, Bury St Edmunds, Suffolk
Printed in England by Clays Ltd, St Ives plc

ISBN-13: 978-0-141-02643-5
ISBN-10: 0-141-02643-X

Contents

Note

These are extracts from *Le Morte D'Arthur*, Sir Thomas Malory's fifteenth-century version of the legend of King Arthur, which recounts Arthur's birth, his ascendancy to the throne after claiming the sword Excalibur, his disastrous marriage to Guenever and the adventures of the Knights of the Round Table. Weaving together adventure, violence, love and enchantment, Malory's enthralling story remains the most magnificent retelling of the Arthurian legend in English.

Book I

First, How Uther Pendragon sent for the Duke of Cornwall and Igraine his wife, and of their departing suddenly again

It befell in the days of Uther Pendragon, when he was king of all England, and so reigned, that there was a mighty duke in Cornwall that held war against him long time. And the duke was called the Duke of Tintagel. And so by means King Uther sent for this duke, charging him to bring his wife with him, for she was called a fair lady, and a passing wise, and her name was called Igraine.

So when the duke and his wife were comen unto the king, by the means of great lords they were accorded both. The king liked and loved this lady well, and he made them great cheer out of measure, and desired to have lain by her. But she was a passing good woman, and would not assent unto the king. And then she told the duke her husband, and said, 'I suppose that we were sent for that I should be dishonoured, wherefore, husband, I counsel you that we depart from hence suddenly, that we may ride all night unto our own castle.' And in like wise as she said so they departed, that neither the king nor none of his council were ware of their departing.

As soon as King Uther knew of their departing so suddenly, he was wonderly wroth. Then he called to him his privy council, and told them of the sudden departing of the duke and his wife. Then they advised the king to send for the duke and his wife by a great charge: 'And if he will not come at your summons, then may ye do your best, then have ye cause to make mighty war upon him.'

So that was done, and the messengers had their answers, and that was this shortly, that neither he nor his wife would not come at him. Then was the king wonderly wroth. And then the king sent him plain word again, and bad him be ready and stuff him and garnish him, for within forty days he would fetch him out of the biggest castle that he hath.

When the duke had this warning, anon he went and furnished and garnished two strong castles of his, of the which the one hight Tintagel, and the other castle hight Terrabil. So his wife Dame Igraine he put in the Castle of Tintagel, and himself he put in the Castle of Terrabil, the which had many issues and posterns out. Then in all haste came Uther with a great host, and laid a siege about the Castle of Terrabil. And there he pitched many pavilions, and there was great war made on both parties, and much people slain.

Then for pure anger and for great love of fair Igraine the King Uther fell sick. So came to the King Uther Sir Ulfius, a noble knight, and asked the king why he was sick.

'I shall tell thee,' said the king. 'I am sick for anger and for love of fair Igraine that I may not be whole.'

'Well, my lord,' said Sir Ulfius, 'I shall seek Merlin, and he shall do you remedy, that your heart shall be pleased.'

So Ulfius departed, and by adventure he met Merlin in a beggar's array, and there Merlin asked Ulfius whom he sought. And he said he had little ado to tell him.

'Well,' said Merlin, 'I know whom thou seekest, for thou seekest Merlin; therefore seek no farther, for I am he, and if King Uther will well reward me, and be sworn unto me to fulfil my desire, that shall be his honour and profit more than mine, for I shall cause him to have all his desire.'

'All this will I undertake,' said Ulfius, 'that there shall be nothing reasonable but thou shalt have thy desire.'

'Well,' said Merlin, 'he shall have his intent and desire. And therefore,' said Merlin, 'ride on your way, for I will not be long behind.'

CHAPTER 2:
How Uther Pendragon made war on the Duke of Cornwall, and how by the mean of Merlin he lay by the Duchess and gat Arthur

Then Ulfius was glad, and rode on more than a pace till that he came to King Uther Pendragon, and told him he had met with Merlin.

'Where is he?' said the king.

'Sir,' said Ulfius, 'he will not dwell long.'

Therewithal Ulfius was ware where Merlin stood at the porch of the pavilion's door. And then Merlin was bound to come to the king. When King Uther saw him, he said he was welcome.

'Sir,' said Merlin 'I know all your heart every deal. So ye will be sworn unto me as ye be a true king anointed, to fulfil my desire, ye shall have your desire.'

Then the king was sworn upon the four Evangelists.

'Sir,' said Merlin, 'this is my desire: the first night that ye shall lie by Igraine ye shall get a child on her, and when that is born, that it shall be delivered to me for to nourish there as I will have it; for it shall be your worship, and the child's avail as mickle as the child is worth.'

'I will well,' said the king, 'as thou wilt have it.'

'Now make you ready,' said Merlin, 'this night ye shall lie with Igraine in the Castle of Tintagel, and ye shall be like the duke her husband, Ulfius shall be like Sir Brastias, a knight of the duke's, and I will be like a knight that hight Sir Jordans, a knight of the duke's. But wait ye make not many questions with her nor her men, but say ye are diseased, and so hie you to bed, and rise not on the morn till I come to you, for the Castle of Tintagel is but ten miles hence.'

So this was done as they devised. But the Duke of Tintagel espied how the king rode from the siege of Terrabil, and therefore that night he issued out of the castle at a postern for to have distressed the king's host. And so, through his own issue, the duke himself was slain or-ever the king came at the Castle of Tintagel.

So after the death of the duke, King Uther lay with Igraine more than three hours after his death, and begat on her that night Arthur; and, or day came, Merlin came to the king, and bad him make him ready, and so he kissed the lady Igraine and departed in all haste. But when the lady heard tell of the duke her husband, and by all record he was dead or-ever King Uther came to her, then she marvelled who that might be that lay with her in likeness of her lord; so she mourned privily and held her peace.

Then all the barons by one assent prayed the king of accord betwixt the lady Igraine and him; the king gave them leave, for fain would he have been accorded with her. So the king put all the trust in Ulfius to entreat between them, so by the entreaty at the last the king and she met together.

'Now will we do well,' said Ulfius. 'Our king is a lusty knight and wifeless, and my lady Igraine is a passing fair lady; it were great joy unto us all, and it might please the king to make her his queen.'

Unto that they all well accorded and moved it to the king. And anon, like a lusty knight, he assented thereto with good will, and so in all haste they were married in a morning with great mirth and joy.

And King Lot of Lothian and of Orkney then wedded Margawse that was Gawain's mother, and King Nentres of the land of Garlot wedded Elaine. All this was done at the request of King Uther. And the third sister Morgan le Fay was put to school in a nunnery, and there she learned so much that she was a great clerk of necromancy, and after she was wedded to King Uriens of the land of Gore, that was Sir Uwain's le Blanchemains father.

CHAPTER 3:
Of the birth of King Arthur and of his nurture

Then Queen Agraine waxed daily greater and greater, so it befell after within half a year, as King Uther lay by his queen, he asked her, by the faith she ought to him, whose was the child within her body; then was she sore abashed to give answer.

'Dismay you not,' said the king, 'but tell me the truth, and I shall love you the better, by the faith of my body.'

'Sir,' said she, 'I shall tell you the truth. The same night that my lord was dead, the hour of his death, as his knights record, there came into my castle of Tintagel a man like my lord in speech and in countenance, and two knights with him in likeness of his two knights Brastias and Jordans, and so I went unto bed with him as I ought to do with my lord, and the same night, as I shall answer unto God, this child was begotten upon me.'

'That is truth,' said the king, 'as ye say; for it was I myself that came in the likeness, and therefore dismay you not, for I am father to the child;' and there he told her all the cause, how it was by Merlin's counsel. Then the queen made great joy when she knew who was the father of her child.

Soon came Merlin unto the king, and said, 'Sir, ye must purvey you for the nourishing of your child.'

'As thou wilt,' said the king, 'be it.'

'Well,' said Merlin, 'I know a lord of yours in this land, that is a passing true man and a faithful, and he shall have the nourishing of your child; and his name is Sir

Ector, and he is a lord of fair livelihood in many parts in England and Wales; and this lord, Sir Ector, let him be sent for, for to come and speak with you, and desire him yourself, as he loveth you, that he will put his own child to nourishing to another woman, and that his wife nourish yours. And when the child is born let it be delivered to me at yonder privy postern unchristened.'

So like as Merlin devised it was done. And when Sir Ector was come he made fiance to the king for to nourish the child like as the king desired; and there the king granted Sir Ector great rewards. Then when the lady was delivered, the king commanded two knights and two ladies to take the child, bound in a cloth of gold, 'and that ye deliver him to what poor man ye meet at the postern gate of the castle.' So the child was delivered unto Merlin, and so he bare it forth unto Sir Ector, and made an holy man to christen him, and named him Arthur; and so Sir Ector's wife nourished him with her own pap.

CHAPTER 4:
Of the death of King Uther Pendragon

Then within two years King Uther fell sick of a great malady. And in the meanwhile his enemies usurped upon him, and did a great battle upon his men, and slew many of his people.

'Sir,' said Merlin, 'ye may not lie so as ye do, for ye must to the field though ye ride on an horse-litter; for ye shall never have the better of your enemies but if your person be there, and then shall ye have the victory.'

So it was done as Merlin had devised, and they carried the king forth in an horse-litter with a great host toward his enemies. And at St Albans there met with the king a great host of the north. And that day Sir Ulfius and Sir Brastias did great deeds of arms, and King Uther's men overcame the northern battle and slew many people, and put the remnant to flight. And then the king returned unto London, and made great joy of his victory.

And then he fell passing sore sick, so that three days and three nights he was speechless; wherefore all the barons made great sorrow, and asked Merlin what counsel were best.

'There nis none other remedy,' said Merlin, 'but God will have his will. But look ye all, barons, be before King Uther to-morn, and God and I shall make him to speak.'

So on the morn all the barons with Merlin came tofore the king; then Merlin said aloud unto King Uther, 'Sir, shall your son Arthur be king, after your days, of this realm with all the appurtenance?'

Then Uther Pendragon turned him, and said in hearing of them all, 'I give him God's blessing and mine, and bid him pray for my soul, and righteously and worshipfully that he claim the crown upon forfeiture of my blessing.' And therewith he yielded up the ghost, and then was he interred as longed to a king, wherefore the queen, fair Igraine, made great sorrow, and all the barons.

CHAPTER 5:
How Arthur was chosen king, and of wonders and marvels of a sword taken out of a stone by the said Arthur

Then stood the realm in great jeopardy long while, for every lord that was mighty of men made him strong, and many weened to have been king. Then Merlin went to the Archbishop of Canterbury, and counselled him for to send for all the lords of the realm, and all the gentlemen of arms, that they should to London come by Christmas, upon pain of cursing; and for this cause: that Jehu, that was born on that night, that He would of his great mercy show some miracle, as He was come to be king of mankind, for to show some miracle who should be rightwise king of this realm. So the Archbishop, by the advice of Merlin, sent for all the lords and gentlemen of arms that they should come by Christmas even unto London. And many of them made them clean of their life, that their prayer might be the more acceptable unto God.

So in the greatest church of London (whether it were Paul's or not the French book maketh no mention) all the estates were long or day in the church for to pray. And when matins and the first mass was done, there was seen in the churchyard, against the high altar, a great stone four square, like unto a marble stone, and in midst thereof was like an anvil of steel a foot on high, and therein stuck a fair sword naked by the point, and letters there were written in gold about the sword that saiden

thus: — WHOSO PULLETH OUT THIS SWORD OF THIS STONE
AND ANVIL, IS RIGHTWISE KING BORN OF ALL ENGLAND.
Then the people marvelled, and told it to the Archbishop.

'I command,' said the Archbishop, 'that ye keep you
within your church, and pray unto God still; that no man
touch the sword till the high mass be all done.'

So when all masses were done all the lords went to
behold the stone and the sword. And when they saw the
scripture, some assayed, such as would have been king.
But none might stir the sword nor move it.

'He is not here,' said the Archbishop, 'that shall
achieve the sword, but doubt not God will make him
known. But this is my counsel,' said the Archbishop,
'that we let purvey ten knights, men of good fame, and
they to keep this sword.'

So it was ordained, and then there was made a cry,
that every man should assay that would, for to win the
sword. And upon New Year's Day the barons let make
a jousts and a tournament, that all knights that would
joust or tourney there might play. And all this was
ordained for to keep the lords together and the commons, for the Archbishop trusted that God would make
him known that should win the sword.

So upon New Year's Day, when the service was done,
the barons rode unto the field, some to joust and some
to tourney, and so it happed that Sir Ector, that had great
livelihood about London, rode unto the jousts, and with
him rode Sir Kay his son, and young Arthur that was his
nourished brother; and Sir Kay was made knight at All
Hallowmass afore. So as they rode to the jousts-ward,
Sir Kay had lost his sword, for he had left it at his father's

lodging, and so he prayed young Arthur for to ride for his sword.

'I will well,' said Arthur, and rode fast after the sword. And when he came home the lady and all were out to see the jousting.

Then was Arthur wroth, and said to himself, 'I will ride to the churchyard, and take the sword with me that sticketh in the stone, for my brother Sir Kay shall not be without a sword this day.' So when he came to the churchyard, Sir Arthur alit and tied his horse to the stile, and so he went to the tent, and found no knights there, for they were at jousting; and so he handled the sword by the handles, and lightly and fiercely pulled it out of the stone, and took his horse and rode his way until he came to his brother Sir Kay, and delivered him the sword.

And as soon as Sir Kay saw the sword, he wist well it was the sword of the stone, and so he rode to his father Sir Ector, and said; 'Sir, lo here is the sword of the stone, wherefore I must be king of this land.'

When Sir Ector beheld the sword, he returned again and came to the church, and there they alit all three, and went into the church. And anon he made Sir Kay to swear upon a book how he came to that sword.

'Sir,' said Sir Kay, 'by my brother Arthur, for he brought it to me.'

'How gat ye this sword?' said Sir Ector to Arthur.

'Sir, I will tell you. When I came home for my brother's sword, I found nobody at home to deliver me his sword, and so I thought my brother Sir Kay should not be swordless, and so I came hither eagerly and pulled it out of the stone without any pain.'

'Found ye any knights about this sword?' said Sir Ector.

'Nay,' said Arthur.

'Now,' said Sir Ector to Arthur, 'I understand ye must be king of this land.'

'Wherefore I,' said Arthur, 'and for what cause?'

'Sir,' said Ector, 'for God will have it so, for there should never man have drawn out this sword, but he that shall be rightwise king of this land. Now let me see whether ye can put the sword there as it was, and pull it out again.'

'That is no mastery,' said Arthur, and so he put it in the stone; therewithal Sir Ector assayed to pull out the sword and failed.

[. . .]

CHAPTER 7:

How King Arthur was crowned, and how he made officers

And at the feast of Pentecost all manner of men assayed to pull at the sword that would assay, but none might prevail but Arthur, and pulled it out afore all the lords and commons that were there, wherefore all the commons cried at once, 'We will have Arthur unto our king; we will put him no more in delay, for we all see that it is God's will that he shall be our king, and who that holdeth against it, we will slay him.' And therewithal they kneeled at once, both rich and poor, and cried

Arthur mercy because they had delayed him so long. And Arthur forgave them, and took the sword between both his hands, and offered it upon the altar where the Archbishop was, and so was he made knight of the best man that was there.

And so anon was the coronation made. And there was he sworn unto his lords and the commons for to be a true king, to stand with true justice from thenceforth the days of this life. Also then he made all lords that held of the crown to come in, and to do service as they ought to do. And many complaints were made unto Sir Arthur of great wrongs that were done since the death of King Uther, of many lands that were bereaved lords, knights, ladies, and gentlemen. Wherefore King Arthur made the lands to be given again unto them that ought them. When this was done, that the king had stablished all the countries about London, then he let make Sir Kay Seneschal of England; and Sir Baudwin of Britain was made constable; and Sir Ulfius was made chamberlain; and Sir Brastias was made warden to wait upon the north from Trent forwards, for it was that time the most part the king's enemies. But within few years after, Arthur won all the north, Scotland, and all that were under their obeissance. Also Wales, a part of it, held against Arthur, but he overcame them all, as he did the remnant, through the noble prowess of himself and his knights of the Round Table.

Book II

*Of a damosel which came girt with a sword for to find
a man of such virtue to draw it out of the scabbard*

After the death of Uther Pendragon reigned Arthur
his son, the which had great war in his days for to get
all England into his hand. For there were many kings
within the realm of England, and in Wales, Scotland, and
Cornwall.

So it befell on a time when King Arthur was at London,
there came a knight and told the king tidings how that
the King Rience of North Wales had reared a great
number of people, and were entered into the land, and
burnt and slew the king's true liege people.

'If this be true,' said Arthur, 'it were great shame unto
mine estate but that he were mightily withstood.'

'It is truth,' said the knight, 'for I saw the host myself.'

'Well,' said the king, 'let make a cry, that all the lords,
knights, and gentlemen of arms should draw unto a
castle' (called Camelot in those days) 'and there the king
would let make a council-general and a great jousts.'

So when the king was come thither with all his baron-
age, and lodged as they seemed best, there was come a
damosel the which was sent on message from the great
lady Lile of Avelion. And when she came before King

Arthur, she told from whom she came, and how she was sent on message unto him for these causes. Then she let her mantle fall that was richly furred; and then was she girt with a noble sword whereof the king had marvel, and said, 'Damosel, for what cause are ye girt with that sword? It beseemeth you not.'

'Now shall I tell you,' said the damosel. 'This sword that I am girt withal doth me great sorrow and cumberance, for I may not be delivered of this sword but by a knight, but he must be a passing good man of his hands and of his deeds, and without villainy or treachery, and without treason. And if I may find such a knight that hath all these virtues, he may draw out this sword out of the sheath, for I have been at King Rience's, it was told me there were passing good knights, and he and all his knights have assayed it and none can speed.'

'This is a great marvel,' said Arthur, 'if this be sooth; I will myself assay to draw out the sword, not presuming upon myself that I am the best knight, but that I will begin to draw at your sword in giving example to all the barons that they shall assay every each one after other when I have assayed it.'

Then Arthur took the sword by the sheath and by the girdle and pulled at it eagerly, but the sword would not out.

'Sir,' said the damosel, 'you need not to pull half so hard, for he that shall pull it out shall do it with little might.'

'Ye say well,' said Arthur; 'now assay ye all my barons.'

'But beware ye be not defiled with shame, treachery ne guile; then it will not avail,' said the damosel, 'for he

16

must be a clean knight without villainy, and of a gentle strain of father side and mother side.'

Most of all the barons of the Round Table that were there at that time assayed all by row, but there might none speed; wherefore the damosel made great sorrow out of measure, and said, 'Alas; I weened in this court had been the best knights without treachery or treason.'

'By my faith,' saith Arthur, 'here are good knights, as I deem, as any be in the world, but their grace is not to help you, wherefore I am displeased.'

CHAPTER 2:
How Balin, arrayed like a poor knight, pulled out the sword, which afterward was cause of his death

Then fell it so that time there was a poor knight with King Arthur, that had been prisoner with him half a year and more for slaying of a knight, the which was cousin unto King Arthur. The name of this knight was called Balin, and by good means of the barons he was delivered out of prison, for he was a good man named of his body, and he was born in Northumberland; and so he went privily into the court, and saw this adventure, whereof it raised his heart, and would assay it as other knights did, but for he was poor and poorly arrayed he put him not far in press; but in his heart he was fully assured to do as well, if his grace happed him, as any knight that there was. And as the damosel took her leave of Arthur and of all the barons, so departing, this knight Balin called unto her, and said,

'Damosel, I pray you of your courtesy, suffer me as

well to assay as these lords; though that I be so poorly clothed, in my heart meseemeth I am fully assured as some of these other, and meseemeth in my heart to speed right well.'

The damosel beheld the poor knight, and saw he was a likely man, but for his poor arrayment she thought he should be of no worship without villainy or treachery. And then she said unto the knight, 'Sir, it needeth not to put me to more pain or labour, for it seemeth not you to speed thereas other have failed.'

'Ah! fair damosel,' said Balin, 'worthiness, and good tatches, and good deeds, are not only in arrayment, but manhood and worship is hid within man's person, and many a worshipful knight is not known unto all people, and therefore worship and hardiness is not in arrayment.'

'By God,' said the damosel, 'ye say sooth; therefore ye shall assay to do what ye may.'

Then Balin took the sword by the girdle and sheath, and drew it out easily; and when he looked on the sword it pleased him much. Then had the king and all the barons great marvel that Balin had done that adventure; many knights had great despite at Balin.

'Certes,' said the damosel, 'this is a passing good knight, and the best that ever I found, and most of worship without treason, treachery, or villainy, and many marvels shall he do. Now, gentle and courteous knight, give me the sword again.'

'Nay,' said Balin, 'for this sword will I keep, but it be taken from me with force.'

'Well,' said the damosel, 'ye are not wise to keep the sword from me, for ye shall slay with the sword the best friend that ye have, and the man that ye most love in the world, and the sword shall be your destruction.'

'I shall take the adventure,' said Balin, 'that God will ordain me, but the sword ye shall not have at this time, by the faith of my body.'

'Ye shall repent it within short time,' said the damosel, 'for I would have the sword more for your avail than for mine, for I am passing heavy for your sake; for ye will not believe that sword shall be your destruction, and that is great pity.' With that the damosel departed, making great sorrow.

Anon after, Balin sent for his horse and armour, and so would depart from the court, and took his leave of King Arthur.

'Nay,' said the king, 'I suppose ye will not depart so lightly from this fellowship, I suppose ye are displeased that I have showed you unkindness. Blame me the less, for I was misinformed against you, but I weened ye had not been such a knight as ye are of worship and prowess, and if ye will abide in this court among my fellowship, I shall so advance you as ye shall be pleased.'

'God thank your highness,' said Balin, 'your bounty and highness may no man praise half to the value; but at this time I must needs depart, beseeching you alway of your good grace.'

'Truly,' said the king, 'I am right wroth for your departing; I pray you, fair knight, that ye tarry not long, and ye shall be right welcome to me, and to my barons, and I shall amend all miss that I have done against you.'

'God thank your great lordship,' said Balin, and therewith made him ready to depart.

Then the most part of the knights of the Round Table said that Balin did not this adventure all only by might, but by witchcraft.

CHAPTER 3:

How the Lady of the Lake demanded the knight's head that had won the sword, or the maiden's head

The meanwhile that this knight was making him ready to depart, there came into the court a lady that hight the Lady of the Lake. And she came on horseback, richly beseen, and saluted King Arthur, and there asked him a gift that he promised her when she gave him the sword.

'That is sooth,' said Arthur, 'a gift I promised you, but I have forgotten the name of my sword that ye gave me.'

'The name of it,' said the lady, 'is Excalibur, that is as much to say as Cut-steel.'

'Ye say well,' said the king, 'ask what ye will and ye shall have it, and it lie in my power to give it.'

'Well,' said the lady, 'I ask the head of the knight that hath won the sword, or else the damosel's head that brought it; I take no force though I have both their heads, for he slew my brother, a good knight and a true, and that gentlewoman was causer of my father's death.'

'Truly,' said King Arthur, 'I may not grant neither of their heads with my worship, therefore ask what ye will else, and I shall fulfil your desire.'

'I will ask none other thing,' said the lady.

When Balin was ready to depart, he saw the Lady of the Lake, that by her means had slain Balin's mother, and he had sought her three years; and when it was told him that she asked his head of King Arthur, he went to her straight and said, 'Evil be you found; ye would have my head, and therefore ye shall lose yours,' and with his sword lightly he smote off her head before King Arthur.

'Alas, for shame!' said Arthur. 'Why have ye done so? Ye have shamed me and all my court, for this was a lady that I was beholden to, and hither she came under my safe-conduct; I shall never forgive you that trespass.'

'Sir,' said Balin, 'me forthinketh of your displeasure, for this same lady was the untruest lady living, and by enchantment and sorcery she hath been the destroyer of many good knights, and she was causer that my mother was burnt, through her falsehood and treachery.'

'What cause soever ye had,' said Arthur, 'ye should have forborne her in my presence; therefore, think not the contrary, ye shall repent it, for such another despite had I never in my court; therefore withdraw you out of my court in all haste that ye may.'

Then Balin took up the head of the lady, and bare it with him to his hostelry, and there he met with his squire, that was sorry he had displeased King Arthur, and so they rode forth out of the town.

'Now,' said Balin, 'we must depart. Take thou this head and bear it to my friends, and tell them how I have sped, and tell my friends in Northumberland that my most foe is dead. Also tell them how I am out of prison, and what adventure befell me at the getting of this sword.'

'Alas!' said the squire, 'ye are greatly to blame for to displease King Arthur.'

'As for that,' said Balin, 'I will hie me in all the haste that I may to meet with King Rience and destroy him, either else to die therefore; and if it may hap me to win him, then will King Arthur be my good and gracious lord.'

'Where shall I meet with you?' said the squire.

'In King Arthur's court,' said Balin. So his squire and he departed at that time.

Then King Arthur and all the court made great dole and had shame of the death of the Lady of the Lake. Then the king buried her richly.

CHAPTER 4:
How Merlin told the adventure of this damosel

At that time there was a knight, the which was the King's son of Ireland, and his name was Lanceor, the which was an orgulous knight, and counted himself one of the best of the court, and he had great despite at Balin for the achieving of the sword, that any should be accounted more hardy, or more of prowess. And he asked King Arthur if he would give him leave to ride after Balin and to revenge the despite that he had done.

'Do your best,' said Arthur, 'I am right wroth with Balin; I would he were quit of the despite that he hath done to me and to my court.'

Then this Lanceor went to his hostelry to make him ready. In the meanwhile came Merlin unto the court of King Arthur, and there was told him the adventure of the sword, and the death of the Lady of the Lake.

'Now shall I say you,' said Merlin, 'this same damosel that here standeth, that brought the sword unto your court, I shall tell you the cause of her coming: she was the falsest damosel that liveth.'

'Say not so,' said they.

'She hath a brother, a passing good knight of prowess and a full true man; and this damosel loved another knight that held her to paramour. And this good knight her brother met with the knight that held her to paramour, and slew him by force of his hands. When this false damosel understood this, she went to the Lady Lile of Avelion, and besought her of help, to be avenged on her own brother.'

CHAPTER 5:
How Balin was pursued by Sir Lanceot, knight of Ireland, and how he jousted and slew him

'And so this Lady Lile of Avelion took her this sword that she brought with her, and told there should no man pull it out of the sheath but if he be one of the best knights of this realm, and he should be hard and full of prowess, and with that sword he should slay her brother. This was the cause that the damosel came into this court. I know it as well as ye. Would God she had not comen into this court, but she came never in fellowship of worship to do good, but always great harm. And that knight that hath achieved the sword shall be destroyed by that sword, for the which will be great damage for there liveth not a knight of more prowess than he is, and he shall do unto you, my lord Arthur, great honour and kindness; and it is great pity he shall not endure but a while, for of his strength and hardiness I know not his match living.'

So the knight of Ireland armed him at all points, and dressed his shield on his shoulder, and mounted upon horseback, and took his spear in his hand, and rode after a great pace, as much as his horse might go. And within a little space on a mountain he had a sight of Balin, and with a loud voice he cried, 'Abide, knight, for ye shall abide whether ye will or nill, and the shield that is tofore you shall not help.'

When Balin heard the noise, he turned his horse fiercely, and said, 'Fair knight, what will ye with me, will ye joust with me?'

'Yea,' said the Irish knight, 'therefore come I after you.'

'Peradventure,' said Balin, 'it had been better to have held you at home, for many a man weeneth to put his enemy to a rebuke, and oft it falleth to himself. Of what court be ye sent from?' said Balin.

'I am come from the court of King Arthur,' said the knight of Ireland, 'that come hither for to revenge the despite ye did this day to King Arthur and to his court.'

'Well,' said Balin, 'I see well I must have ado with you; that me forthinketh for to grieve King Arthur, or any of his court; and your quarrel is full simple,' said Balin, 'unto me, for the lady that is dead did me great damage, and else would I have been loth as any knight that liveth for to slay a lady.'

'Make you ready,' said the knight Lanceor, 'and dress you unto me, for that one shall abide in the field.'

Then they took their spears, and came together as much as their horses might drive, and the Irish knight smote Balin on the shield, that all went shivers of his spear, and Balin hit him through the shield, and the hauberk perished, and so pierced through his body and the horse's croup, and anon turned his horse fiercely, and drew out his sword, and wist not that he had slain him; and then he saw him lie as a dead corpse.

[. . .]

CHAPTER 10:
How King Arthur had a battle against Nero and King Lot of Orkney, and how King Lot was deceived by Merlin, and how twelve kings were slain

Then King Arthur made ready his host in ten battles, and Nero was ready in the field afore the Castle Terrabil with a great host, and he had ten battles, with many more people than Arthur had. Then Nero had the vanguard with the most part of his people. And Merlin came to King Lot of the Isle of Orkney, and held him with a tale of prophecy, till Nero and his people were destroyed. And there Sir Kay the Seneschal did passingly well, that the days of his life the worship went never from him; and Sir Hervis de Revel did marvellous deeds with King Arthur, and King Arthur slew that day twenty knights and maimed forty. At that time came in the Knight with the Two Swords and his brother Balan, but they two did so marvellously that the king and all the knights marvelled of them, and all they that beheld them said they were sent from heaven as angels, or devils from hell; and King Arthur said himself they were the best knights that ever he saw, for they gave such strokes that all men had wonder of them.

In the meanwhile came one to King Lot, and told him while he tarried there Nero was destroyed and slain with all his people.

'Alas,' said King Lot, 'I am ashamed, for by my default there is many a worshipful man slain, for and we had been together there had been none host under the heaven that had been able for to have matched with us; this faiter with his prophecy hath mocked me.'

(All that did Merlin, for he knew well that and King Lot had been with his body there at the first battle, King Arthur had been slain, and all his people destroyed; and well Merlin knew the one of the kings should be dead that day, and loth was Merlin that any of them both should be slain; but of the twain, he had lever King Lot had been slain than King Arthur.)

'Now what is best to do?' said King Lot of Orkney. 'Whether is me better to treat with King Arthur or to fight, for the greater part of our people are slain and destroyed?'

'Sir,' said a knight, 'set on Arthur for they are weary and forfoughten and we be fresh.'

'As for me,' said King Lot, 'I would every knight would do his part as I would do mine.'

And then they advanced banners and smote together and all to-shivered their spears; and Arthur's knights, with the help of the Knight with the Two Swords and his brother Balan put King Lot and his host to the worse. But always King Lot held him in the foremost front, and did marvellous deeds of arms, for all his host was borne up by his hands, for he abode all knights. Alas he might not endure, the which was great pity, that so worthy a knight as he was one should be overmatched, that of late time afore had been a knight of King Arthur's, and wedded the sister of King Arthur; and for King Arthur lay by King Lot's wife, the which was Arthur's sister, and gat on her Mordred, therefore King Lot held against Arthur.

So there was a knight that was called the Knight with the Strange Beast, and at that time his right name was called Pellinor, the which was a good man of prowess, and he smote a mighty stroke at King Lot as he fought with all his enemies, and he failed of his stroke, and smote the horse's neck, that he fell to the ground with King Lot; and therewith anon Pellinor smote him a great stroke through the helm and head unto the brows. And then all the host of Orkney fled for the death of King Lot, and there were slain many mothers' sons. But King Pellinor bare the wite of the death of King Lot, wherefore Sir Gawain revenged the death of his father the tenth year after he was made knight, and slew King Pellinor with his own hands.

Also there were slain at that battle twelve kings on the side of King Lot with Nero, and all were buried in the Church of Saint Stephen's in Camelot, and the remnant of knights and of other were buried in a great rock.

CHAPTER II:
Of the interment of twelve kings, and of the prophecy of Merlin how Balin should give the Dolorous Stroke

So at the interment came King Lot's wife Margawse with her four sons, Gawain, Agravain, Gaheris, and Gareth. Also there came thither King Uriens, Sir Uwain's father, and Morgan le Fay his wife that was King Arthur's sister. All these came to the interment.

But of all these twelve kings, King Arthur let make the tomb of King Lot passing richly, and made his tomb by his own; and then Arthur let make twelve images of laton and copper, and over-gilt it with gold, in the sign of twelve kings, and each one of them held a taper of wax that burnt day and night; and King Arthur was made in sign of a figure standing above them with a sword drawn in his hand, and all the twelve figures had countenance like unto men that were overcome.

All this made Merlin by his subtle craft, and there he told the king, 'When I am dead these tapers shall burn no longer, and soon after the adventures of the Sangrail shall come among you and be achieved.' Also he told Arthur how 'Balin the worshipful knight shall give the Dolorous Stroke, whereof shall fall great vengeance.'

'Oh, where is Balin and Balan and Pellinor?' said King Arthur.

'As for Pellinor,' said Merlin, 'he will meet with you soon; and as for Balin he will not be long from you; but the other brother will depart, ye shall see him no more.'

'By my faith,' said Arthur, 'they are two marvellous knights, and namely Balin passeth of prowess of any knight that ever I found, for much beholden I am unto him; would God he would abide with me.'

'Sir,' said Merlin, 'look ye keep well the scabbard of Excalibur, for ye shall lose no blood while ye have the scabbard upon you, though ye have as many wounds upon you as ye may have.' (So after, for great trust, Arthur betook the scabbard to Morgan le Fay his sister, and she loved another knight better than her husband King Uriens or King Arthur, and she would have had Arthur her brother slain, and therefore she let make another scabbard like it by enchantment, and gave the scabbard Excalibur to her love; and the knight's name was called Accolon, that after had near slain King Arthur.) After this Merlin told unto King Arthur of the prophecy that there should be a great battle beside Salisbury, and Mordred his own son should be against him. Also he told him that Bagdemagus was his cousin, and germain unto King Uriens.

CHAPTER 12:

How a sorrowful knight came tofore Arthur, and how Balin fetched him, and how that knight was slain by a knight invisible

Within a day or two King Arthur was somewhat sick, and he let pitch his pavilion in a meadow, and there he laid him down on a pallet to sleep, but he might have no rest. Right so he heard a great noise of an horse, and therewith the king looked out at the porch of the pavilion, and saw a knight coming even by him making great dole.

'Abide, fair sir,' said Arthur, 'and tell me wherefore thou makest this sorrow.'

'Ye may little amend me,' said the knight, and so passed forth to the Castle of Meliot.

Anon after there came Balin, and when he saw King Arthur he alit off his horse, and came to the king on foot, and saluted him.

'By my head,' said Arthur, 'ye be welcome. Sir, right now came riding this way a knight making great mourn, for what cause I cannot tell; wherefore I would desire of you of your courtesy and of your gentleness to fetch again that knight either by force or else by his good will.'

'I will do more for your lordship than that,' said Balin; and so he rode more than a pace, and found the knight with a damosel in a forest, and said, 'Sir knight, ye must come with me unto King Arthur, for to tell him of your sorrow.'

'That will I not,' said the knight, 'for it will scathe me greatly, and do you none avail.'

'Sir,' said Balin, 'I pray you make you ready, for ye must go with me, or else I must fight with you and bring you by force, and that were me loth to do.'

'Will ye be my warrant,' said the knight, 'and I go with you?'

'Yea,' said Balin, 'or else I will die therefore.'

And so he made him ready to go with Balin, and left the damosel still. And as they were even afore King Arthur's pavilion, there came one invisible, and smote this knight that went with Balin throughout the body with a spear.

'Alas,' said the knight, 'I am slain under your conduct with a knight called Garlon; therefore take my horse that is better than yours, and ride to the damosel, and follow the quest that I was in as she will lead you, and revenge my death when ye may.'

'That shall I do,' said Balin, 'and that I make a vow unto knighthood;' and so he departed from this knight with great sorrow.

So King Arthur let bury this knight richly, and made a mention on his tomb, how there was slain Herlews le Berbeus, and by whom the treachery was done, the knight Garlon. But ever the damosel bare the truncheon of the spear with her that Sir Herlews was slain withal.

CHAPTER 13:

How Balin and the damosel met with a knight which was in likewise slain, and how the damosel bled for the custom of a castle

So Balin and the damosel rode into a forest, and there met with a knight that had been on hunting, and that knight asked Balin for what cause he made so great sorrow.

'Me list not to tell you,' said Balin.

'Now,' said the knight, 'and I were armed as ye be I would fight with you.'

'That should little need,' said Balin, 'I am not afeared to tell you,' and told him all the cause how it was.

'Ah,' said the knight, 'is this all? Here I ensure you by the faith of my body never to depart from you while my life lasteth.'

And so they went to the hostelry and armed them, and so rode forth with Balin. And as they came by an hermitage even by a churchyard, there came the knight Garlon invisible, and smote this knight, Perin de Mountbeliard, through the body with a spear.

'Alas,' said the knight, 'I am slain by this traitor knight that rideth invisible.'

'Alas,' said Balin, 'it is not the first despite he hath done me.' And there the hermit and Balin buried the knight under a rich stone and a tomb royal.

And on the morn they found letters of gold written, how: SIR GAWAIN SHALL REVENGE HIS FATHER'S DEATH, KING LOT, ON THE KING PELLINOR.

Anon after this Balin and the damosel rode till they came to a castle, and there Balin alit, and he and the damosel went to go into the castle, and anon as Balin came within the castle's gate the portcullis fell down at his back, and there fell many men about the damosel, and would have slain her. When Balin saw that, he was sore aggrieved, for he might not help the damosel; and then he went up into the tower, and leapt over the walls into the ditch, and hurt him not; and anon he pulled out his sword and would have foughten with them. And they all said nay, they would not fight with him, for they did nothing but the old custom of the castle, and told him how their lady was sick, and had lain many years, and she might not be whole but if she had a dish of silver full of blood of a clean maid and a king's daughter; 'and therefore the custom of the castle is, there shall no damosel pass this way but she shall bleed of her blood in a silver dish full.'

'Well,' said Balin, 'she shall bleed as much as she may bleed, but I will not lose the life of her whiles my life lasteth.'

And so Balin made her to bleed by her good will, but her blood halp not the lady. And so he and she rested there all night, and had there right good cheer; and on the morn they passed on their ways. And as it telleth after in the Sangrail, that Sir Percival's sister halp that lady with her blood, whereof she was dead.

CHAPTER 14:
How Balin met with that knight named Garlon at a feast, and there he slew him to have his blood to heal therewith the son of his host

Then they rode three or four days and never met with adventure, and by hap they were lodged with a gentleman that was a rich man and well at ease. And as they sat at their supper Balin heard one complain grievously by him in a chair.

'What is this noise?' said Balin.

'Forsooth,' said his host, 'I will tell you. I was but late at a jousting, and there I jousted with a knight that is brother unto King Pellam, and twice smote I him down, and then he promised to quit me on my best friend; and so he wounded my son, that cannot be whole till I have of that knight's blood, and he rideth alway invisible, but I know not his name.'

'Ah!' said Balin, 'I know that knight, his name is Garlon, he hath slain two knights of mine in the same manner, therefore I had lever meet with that knight than all the gold in this realm, for the despite he hath done me.'

'Well,' said his host, 'I shall tell you, King Pellam of Listinoise hath made do cry in all this country a great feast that shall be within these twenty days, and no knight may come there but if he bring his wife with him, or his paramour; and that knight, your enemy and mine, ye shall see that day.'

'Then I behote you,' said Balin, 'part of his blood to heal your son withal.'

'We will be forward to-morn,' said his host.

So on the morn they rode all three toward Pellam, and they had fifteen days' journey or they came thither; and that same day began the great feast. And so they alit and stabled their horses, and went into the castle; but Balin's host might not be let in because he had no lady.

Then Balin was well received and brought unto a chamber and unarmed him, and there were brought him robes to his pleasure, and would have had Balin leave his sword behind him.

'Nay,' said Balin, 'that do I not, for it is the custom of my country a knight always to keep his weapon with him, and that custom will I keep, or else I will depart as I came.' Then they gave him leave to wear his sword, and so he went unto the castle, and was set among knights of worship, and his lady afore him.

Soon Balin asked a knight, 'Is there not a knight in this court whose name is Garlon?'

'Yonder he goeth,' said a knight, 'he with the black face; he is the marvellest knight that is now living, for he destroyeth many good knights, for he goeth invisible.'

'Ah well,' said Balin, 'is that he?' Then Balin advised him long: 'If I slay him here I shall not scape, and if I leave him now, peradventure I shall never meet with him again at such a steven and much harm he will do and he live.'

Therewith this Garlon espied that this Balin beheld him, and then he came and smote Balin on the face with the back of his hand, and said, 'Knight, why beholdest thou me so? For shame therefore, eat thy meat and do that thou came for.'

'Thou sayest sooth,' said Balin, 'this is not the first despite that thou hast done me, and therefore I will do that I came for,' and rose up fiercely and clave his head to the shoulders. 'Give me the truncheon,' said Balin to his lady, 'wherewith he slew your knight.' Anon she gave it him, for alway she bare the truncheon with her. And therewith Balin smote him through the body, and said openly, 'With that truncheon thou hast slain a good knight, and now it sticketh in thy body.'

And then Balin called unto him his host, saying, 'Now may ye fetch blood enough to heal your son withal.'

CHAPTER 15:
How Balin fought with King Pellam, and how his sword brake, and how he gat a spear wherewith he smote the Dolorous Stroke

Anon all the knights arose from the table for to set on Balin, and King Pellam himself arose up fiercely, and said, 'Knight, hast thou slain my brother? Thou shalt die therefore or thou depart.'

'Well,' said Balin, 'do it yourself.'

'Yes,' said King Pellam, 'there shall no man have ado with thee but myself, for the love of my brother.'

Then King Pellam caught in his hand a grim weapon and smote eagerly at Balin; but Balin put his sword betwixt his head and the stroke, and therewith his sword brast in sunder. And when Balin was weaponless he ran into a chamber for to seek some weapon, and so from chamber to chamber, and no weapon he could find, and always King Pellam after him. And at the last he entered into a chamber that was marvellously well dight and richly, and a bed arrayed with cloth of gold the richest that might be thought, and one lying therein, and thereby stood a table of clean gold with four pillars of silver that bare up the table, and upon the table stood a marvellous spear strangely wrought.

And when Balin saw that spear, he gat it in his hand and turned him to King Pellam, and smote him passingly sore with that spear, that King Pellam fell down in a swoon, and therewith the castle roof and walls brake and fell to the earth, and Balin fell down so that he might not stir foot nor hand. And so the most part of the castle, that was fall down through that Dolorous Stroke, lay upon Pellam and Balin three days.

CHAPTER 16:

How Balin was delivered by Merlin, and saved a knight that would have slain himself for love

Then Merlin came thither and took up Balin, and gat him a good horse, for his was dead, and bad him ride out of that country.

'I would have my damosel,' said Balin.

'Lo,' said Merlin, 'where she lieth dead.'

And King Pellam lay so, many years sore wounded, and might never be whole till Galahad the Haut Prince healed him in the quest of the Sangrail, for in that place was part of the blood of Our Lord Jesus Christ, that Joseph of Arimathea brought into this land, and there himself lay in that rich bed. And that was the same spear that Longius smote Our Lord to the heart. And King Pellam was nigh of Joseph's kin, and that was the most worshipful man that lived in those days, and great pity it was of his hurt, for through that stroke, turned to great dole, tray and tene.

Then departed Balin from Merlin, and said, 'In this world we meet never no more.' So he rode forth through the fair countries and cities, and found the people dead, slain on every side. And all that were alive cried, 'O Balin, thou hast caused great damage in these countries; for the dolorous stroke thou gavest unto King Pellam, three countries are destroyed, and doubt not but the vengeance will fall on thee at the last.'

When Balin was past those countries he was passing fain. So he rode eight days or he met with adventure.

And at the last he came into a fair forest in a valley, and was ware of a tower, and there beside he saw a great horse of war, tied to a tree, and there beside sat a fair knight on the ground and made great mourning, and he was a likely man, and a well made. Balin said, 'God save you, why be ye so heavy? Tell me and I will amend it, and I may to my power.'

'Sir knight,' said he again, 'thou doest me great grief, for I was in merry thoughts, and now thou puttest me to more pain.'

Balin went a little from him, and looked on his horse; then heard Balin him say thus: 'Ah, fair lady, why have ye broken my promise, for thou promisest me to meet me here by noon, and I may curse thee that ever ye gave me this sword, for with this sword I slay myself,' and pulled it out. And therewith Balin start unto him and took him by the hand.

'Let go my hand,' said the knight, 'or else I shall slay thee.'

'That shall not need,' said Balin, 'for I shall promise you my help to get you your lady, and ye will tell me where she is.'

'What is your name?' said the knight.

'My name is Balin le Savage.'

'Ah, sir, I know you well enough, ye are the Knight with the Two Swords, and the man of most prowess of your hands living.'

'What is your name?' said Balin.

'My name is Garnish of the Mount, a poor man's son, but by my prowess and hardiness a duke hath made me knight, and gave me lands; his name is Duke Hermel, and his daughter is she that I love, and she me, as I deemed.'

'How far is she hence?' said Balin.

'But six mile,' said the knight.

'Now ride we hence,' said these two knights. So they rode more than a pace, till that they came to a fair castle well walled and ditched.

'I will into the castle,' said Balin, 'and look if she be there.'

So he went in and searched from chamber to chamber, and found her bed, but she was not there. Then Balin looked into a fair little garden, and under a laurel tree he saw her lie upon a quilt of green samite and a knight in her arms, fast halsing either other, and under their heads grass and herbs. When Balin saw her lie so with the foulest knight that ever he saw, and she a fair lady, then Balin went through all the chambers again, and told the knight how he found her as she had slept fast, and so brought him in the place there she lay fast sleeping.

CHAPTER 17:
How that knight slew his love and a knight lying by her, and after, how he slew himself with his own sword, and how Balin rode toward a castle where he lost his life

And when Garnish beheld her so lying, for pure sorrow his mouth and nose brast out on bleeding, and with his sword he smote off both their heads, and then he made sorrow out of measure, and said, 'O Balin, much sorrow hast thou brought unto me, for haddest thou not showed me that sight I should have passed my sorrow.'

'Forsooth,' said Balin, 'I did it to this intent that it should better thy courage, and that ye might see and know her falsehood, and to cause you to leave love of such a lady; God knoweth I did none other but as I would ye did to me.'

'Alas,' said Garnish, 'now is my sorrow double that I may not endure, now have I slain that I most loved in all my life;' and therewith suddenly he rove himself on his own sword unto the hilts.

When Balin saw that, he dressed him thenceward, lest folk would say he had slain them; and so he rode forth, and within three days he came by a cross, and thereon were letters of gold written, that said, IT IS NOT FOR NO KNIGHT ALONE TO RIDE TOWARD THIS CASTLE.

Then saw he an old hoar gentleman coming toward him, that said, 'Balin le Savage, thou passest thy bounds to come this way, therefore turn again and it will avail thee.' And he vanished away anon; and so he heard an horn blow as it had been the death of a beast. 'That blast,' said Balin, 'is blown for me, for I am the prize and yet am I not dead.'

Anon withal he saw an hundred ladies and many knights, that welcomed him with fair semblant, and made him passing good cheer unto his sight, and led him into the castle, and there was dancing and minstrelsy and all manner of joy. Then the chief lady of the castle said, 'Knight with the Two Swords, ye must have ado and joust with a knight hereby that keepeth an island, for there may no man pass this way, but he must joust or he pass.'

'That is an unhappy custom,' said Balin, 'that a knight may not pass this way but if he joust.'

'Ye shall not have ado but with one knight,' said the lady.

'Well,' said Balin, 'since I shall, thereto I am ready, but travelling men are oft weary and their horses too; but though my horse be weary my heart is not weary. I would be fain there my death should be.'

'Sir,' said a knight to Balin, 'methinketh your shield is not good, I will lend you a bigger, thereof I pray you.'

And so he took the shield that was unknown and left his own, and so rode unto the island, and put him and his horse in a great boat; and when he came on the other side he met with a damosel, and she said, 'O knight Balin, why have ye left your own shield? Alas ye have put yourself in great danger, for by your shield ye should have been known; it is great pity of you as ever was of knight, for of thy prowess and hardiness thou hast no fellow living.'

'Me repenteth,' said Balin, 'that ever I came within this country, but I may not turn now again for shame, and what adventure shall fall to me, be it life or death, I will take the adventure that shall come to me.' And then he looked on his armour, and understood he was well armed, and therewith blessed him and mounted upon his horse.

[. . .]

Book III

How King Arthur took a wife, and wedded Guenever,
daughter to Leodegrance, king of the land of
Camelerd, with whom he had the Round Table

In the beginning of Arthur, after he was chosen king by adventure and by grace, for the most part of the barons knew not that he was Uther Pendragon's son, but as Merlin made it openly known, but yet many kings and lords held great war against him for that cause, but well Arthur overcame them all, for the most part the days of his life he was ruled much by the counsel of Merlin. So it fell on a time King Arthur said unto Merlin, 'My barons will let me have no rest, but needs I must take a wife, and I will none take but by thy counsel and by thine advice.'

'It is well done,' said Merlin, 'that ye take a wife, for a man of your bounty and noblesse should not be without a wife. Now is there any that ye love more than another?'

'Yea,' said King Arthur, 'I love Guenever the King's daughter Leodegrance, of the land of Camelerd, the which holdeth in his house the Table Round that ye told he had of my father Uther. And this damosel is the most valiant and fairest lady that I know living, or yet that ever I could find.'

'Sir,' said Merlin, 'as of her beauty and fairness she is one of the fairest alive, but and ye loved her not so well as ye do, I should find you a damosel of beauty and of goodness that should like you and please you, and your heart were not set; but there as a man's heart is set, he will be loth to return.'

'That is truth,' said King Arthur.

But Merlin warned the king covertly that Guenever was not wholesome for him to take to wife, for he warned him that Launcelot should love her, and she him again; and so he turned his tale to the adventures of Sangrail. Then Merlin desired of the king for to have men with him that should enquire of Guenever, and so the king granted him, and Merlin went forth unto King Leodegrance of Camelerd, and told him of the desire of the king that he would have unto his wife Guenever his daughter.

'That is to me,' said King Leodegrance, 'the best tidings that ever I heard, that so worthy a king of prowess and noblesse will wed my daughter. And as for my lands, I will give him, wist I it might please him, but he hath lands enow, him needeth none, but I shall send him a gift shall please him much more, for I shall give him the Table Round, the which Uther Pendragon gave me, and when it is full complete, there is an hundred knights and fifty. And as for an hundred good knights I have myself, but I fault fifty, for so many have been slain in my days.'

And so Leodegrance delivered his daughter Guenever unto Merlin, and the Table Round with the hundred knights, and so they rode freshly, with great royalty, what by water and what by land, till that they came nigh unto London.

CHAPTER 2:

How the knights of the Round Table were ordained and their sieges blessed by the Bishop of Canterbury

When King Arthur heard of the coming of Guenever and the hundred knights with the Table Round, then King Arthur made great joy for her coming, and that rich present, and said openly, 'This fair lady is passing welcome unto me, for I have loved her long, and therefore there is nothing so leve to me. And these knights with the Round Table pleasen me more than right great riches.'

And in all haste the king let ordain for the marriage and the coronation in the most honourable wise that could be devised. 'Now, Merlin,' said King Arthur, 'go thou and espy me in all this land fifty knights which be of most prowess and worship.'

Within short time Merlin had found such knights that should fulfil twenty and eight knights, but no more he could find. Then the Bishop of Canterbury was fetched, and he blessed the sieges with great royalty and devotion, and there set the eight and twenty knights in their sieges.

And when this was done Merlin said, 'Fair sirs, you must all arise and come to King Arthur for to do him homage; he will have the better will to maintain you.'

And so they arose and did their homage, and when they were gone Merlin found in every sieges letters of gold that told the knights' names that had sitten therein. But two sieges were void.

And so anon came young Gawain and asked the king a gift.

'Ask,' said the king, 'and I shall grant it you.'

'Sir, I ask that ye will make me knight that same day ye shall wed fair Guenever.'

'I will do it with a good will,' said King Arthur, 'and do unto you all the worship that I may, for I must by reason ye are mine nephew, my sister's son.'

CHAPTER 3:
How a poor man riding upon a lean mare desired of King Arthur to make his son knight

Forthwithal there came a poor man into the court, and brought with him a fair young man of eighteen year of age riding upon a lean mare; and the poor man asked all men that he met, 'Where shall I find King Arthur?'

'Yonder he is,' said the knights, 'wilt thou anything with him?'

'Yea,' said the poor man, 'therefore I came hither.'

Anon as he came before the king, he saluted him and said, 'O King Arthur, the flower of all knights and kings, I beseech Jesu save thee. Sir, it was told me that at this time of your marriage ye would give any man the gift that he would ask, out except that were unreasonable.'

'That is truth,' said the king, 'such cries I let make, and that will I hold, so it appair not my realm nor mine estate.'

'Ye say well and graciously,' said the poor man. 'Sir, I ask nothing else but that ye will make my son here a knight.'

'It is a great thing thou askest of me,' said the king. 'What is thy name?' said the king to the poor man.

'Sir, my name is Aries the cowherd.'

'Whether cometh this of thee or of thy son?' said the king.

'Nay, sir,' said Aries, 'this desire cometh of my son and not of me, for I shall tell you I have thirteen sons, and all they will fall to what labour I put them, and will be right glad to do labour, but this child will not labour for me, for anything that my wife or I may do, but always he will be shooting or casting darts, and glad for to see battles and to behold knights, and always day and night he desireth of me to be made a knight.'

'What is thy name?' said the king unto the young man.

'Sir, my name is Tor.'

The king beheld him fast, and saw he was passingly well-visaged and passingly well made of his years. 'Well,' said King Arthur unto Aries the cowherd, 'fetch all thy sons afore me that I may see them.'

And so the poor man did, and all were shapen much like the poor man. But Tor was not like none of them all in shape ne in countenance, for he was much more than any of them.

'Now,' said King Arthur unto the cowherd, 'where is the sword he shall be made knight withal?'

'It is here,' said Tor.

'Take it out of the sheath,' said the king, 'and require me to make you a knight.'

Then Tor alit off his mare and pulled out his sword, kneeling, and requiring the king that he would make him knight, and that he might be a knight of the Table Round.

'As for a knight I will make you,' and therewith smote

him in the neck with the sword, saying, 'Be ye a good knight, and so I pray to God so ye may be, and if ye be of prowess and of worthiness ye shall be a knight of the Table Round. Now Merlin,' said Arthur, 'say whether this Tor shall be a good knight or no.'

'Yea, sir, he ought to be a good knight, for he is comen of as good a man as any is alive, and of king's blood.'

'How so, sir?' said the king.

'I shall tell you,' said Merlin. 'This poor man, Aries the cowherd, is not his father, he is nothing sib to him, for King Pellinor is his father.'

'I suppose nay,' said the cowherd.

'Fetch thy wife afore me,' said Merlin, 'and she shall not say nay.'

Anon the wife was fetched, which was a fair housewife, and there she answered Merlin full womanly, and there she told the king and Merlin that when she was a maid, and went to milk kine, there met with her a stern knight, 'and half by force he had my maidenhead, and at that time he begat my son Tor, and he took away from me my greyhound that I had that time with me, and said that he would keep the greyhound for my love.'

'Ah,' said the cowherd, 'I weened not this, but I may believe it well, for he had never no tatches of me.'

'Sir,' said Tor unto Merlin, 'dishonour not my mother.'

'Sir,' said Merlin, 'it is more for your worship than hurt, for your father is a good man and a king, and he may right well advance you and your mother, for ye were begotten or ever she was wedded.'

'That is truth,' said the wife.

'It is the less grief unto me,' said the cowherd.

CHAPTER 4:
How Sir Tor was known for son of King Pellinor, and how Gawain was made knight

So on the morn King Pellinor came to the court of King Arthur, which had great joy of him, and told him of Tor, how he was his son, and how he had made him knight at the request of the cowherd. When Pellinor beheld Tor, he pleased him much. So the king made Gawain knight, but Tor was the first he made at the feast.

'What is the cause,' said King Arthur, 'that there be two places void in the sieges?'

'Sir,' said Merlin, 'there shall no man sit in those places but they shall be of most worship. But in the Siege Perilous there shall no man sit therein but one, and if there be any so hardy to do it he shall be destroyed, and he that shall sit there shall have no fellow.'

And therewith Merlin took King Pellinor by the hand, and in the one hand next the two sieges and the Siege Perilous he said, in open audience, 'This is your place and best ye are worthy to sit therein of any that is here.'

Thereat sat Sir Gawain in great envy and told Gaheris his brother, 'Yonder knight is put to great worship, the which grieveth me sore, for he slew our father King Lot, therefore I will slay him,' said Gawain, 'with a sword that was sent me that is passing trenchant.'

'Ye shall not so,' said Gaheris, 'at this time, for at this time I am but a squire, and when I am made knight I will be avenged on him, and therefore, brother, it is best ye suffer till another time, that we may have him out of the court, for, and we did so we should trouble this high feast.'

'I will well,' said Gawain, 'as ye will.'

CHAPTER 5:

How at the feast of the wedding of King Arthur to Guenever, a white hart came into the hall, and thirty couple hounds, and how a brachet pinched the hart which was taken away

Then was the high feast made ready, and the king was wedded at Camelot unto Dame Guenever in the Church of Saint Stephen's, with great solemnity. And as every man was set after his degree, Merlin went to all the knights of the Round Table, and bad them sit still, that none of them remove, 'for ye shall see a strange and a marvellous adventure.'

Right so as they sat there came running in a white hart into the hall, and a white brachet next him, and thirty couple of black running hounds came after with a great cry, and the hart went about the Table Round as he went by other boards, the white brachet bit him by the buttock and pulled out a piece, wherethrough the hart leapt a great leap and overthrew a knight that sat at the board side, and therewith the knight arose and took up the brachet, and so went forth out of the hall, and took his horse and rode his way with the brachet.

Right so anon came in a lady on a white palfrey, and cried aloud to King Arthur, 'Sir, suffer me not to have this despite, for the brachet was mine that the knight led away.'

'I may not do therewith,' said the king.

With this there came a knight riding all armed on a great horse, and took the lady away with him with force, and ever she cried and made great dole. When she was gone the king was glad, for she made such a noise.

'Nay,' said Merlin, 'ye may not leave these adventures so lightly, for these adventures must be brought again or else it would be disworship to you and to your feast.'

'I will,' said the king, 'that all be done by your advice.'

'Then,' said Merlin, 'let call Sir Gawain, for he must bring again the white hart. Also, sir, ye must let call Sir Tor, for he must bring again the brachet and the knight, or else slay him. Also let call King Pellinor, for he must bring again the lady and the knight, or else slay him. And these three knights shall do marvellous adventures or they come again.'

Then were they called all three as it rehearseth afore, and every each of them took his charge, and armed them surely. But Sir Gawain had the first request, and therefore we will begin at him.

CHAPTER 6:
How Sir Gawain rode for to fetch again the hart, and how two brethren fought each against other for the hart

Sir Gawain rode more than a pace, and Gaheris his brother that rode with him instead of a squire to do him service. So as they rode they saw two knights fight on horseback passing sore, so Sir Gawain and his brother rode betwixt them, and asked them for what cause they fought so.

The one knight answered and said, 'We fight for a simple matter, for we two be two brethren born and begotten of one man and of one woman.'

'Alas,' said Sir Gawain, 'why do ye so?'

'Sir,' said the elder, 'there came a white hart this way this day, and many hounds chased him, and a white brachet was alway next him, and we understood it was adventure made for the high feast of King Arthur, and therefore I would have gone after to have won me worship; and here my younger brother said he would go after the hart, for he was better knight than I; and for this cause we fell at debate, and so we thought to prove which of us both was better knight.'

'This is a simple cause,' said Sir Gawain; 'uncouth men ye should debate withal, and no brother with brother; therefor but if ye will do by my counsel I will have ado with you, that is, ye shall yield you unto me, and that ye go unto King Arthur and yield you unto his grace.'

'Sir knight,' said the two brethren, 'we are forfoughten and much blood have we lost through our wilfulness, and therefore we would be loth to have ado with you.'

'Then do as I will have you,' said Sir Gawain.

'We will agree to fulfil your will; but by whom shall we say that we be thither sent?'

'Ye may say, "by the knight that followeth the quest of the hart that was white." Now what is your name?' said Gawain.

'Sorlouse of the Forest,' said the elder.

'And my name is,' said the younger, 'Brian of the Forest.'

And so they departed and went to the king's court,

and Sir Gawain on his quest. And as Gawain followed the hart by the cry of the hounds, even afore him there was a great river, and the hart swam over; and as Sir Gawain would follow after, there stood a knight over the other side, and said, 'Sir knight, come not over after this hart but if thou wilt joust with me.'

'I will not fail as for that,' said Sir Gawain, 'to follow the quest that I am in,' and so made his horse to swim over the water.

And anon they gat their spears and ran together full hard; but Sir Gawain smote him off his horse, and then he turned his horse and bad him yield him.

'Nay,' said the knight, 'not so, though thou have the better of me on horseback. I pray thee, valiant knight, alight afoot and match we together with swords.'

'What is your name?' said Sir Gawain.

'Alardin of the Isles,' said the other.

Then either dressed their shields and smote together, but Sir Gawain smote him so hard through the helm that it went to the brains, and the knight fell down dead.

'Ah!' said Gaheris, 'that was a mighty stroke of a young knight.'

CHAPTER 7:

How the hart was chased into a castle and there slain, and how Gawain slew a lady

Then Gawain and Gaheris rode more than a pace after the white hart, and let slip at the hart three couple of greyhounds, and so they chase the hart into a castle, and in the chief place of the castle they slew the hart. Sir Gawain and Gaheris followed after. Right so there came a knight out of a chamber with a sword drawn in his hand and slew two of the greyhounds, even in the sight of Sir Gawain, and the remnant he chased them with his sword out of the castle.

And when he came again, he said, 'O my white hart, me repenteth that thou art dead, for my sovereign lady gave thee to me, and evil have I kept thee, and thy death shall be dear bought and I live.'

And anon he went into his chamber and armed him, and came out fiercely, and there met he with Sir Gawain.

'Why have ye slain my hounds?' said Sir Gawain, 'for they did but their kind, and lever I had ye had wroken your anger upon me than upon a dumb beast.'

'Thou sayest truth,' said the knight, 'I have avenged me on thy hounds, and so I will on thee or thou go.'

Then Sir Gawain alit afoot and dressed his shield, and struck together mightily, and clave their shields, and stoned their helms, and brake their hauberks that the blood ran down to their feet. At last Sir Gawain smote the knight so hard that he fell to the earth, and then he cried mercy, and yielded him, and besought him as he was a knight and gentleman, to save his life.

'Thou shalt die,' said Sir Gawain, 'for slaying of my hounds.'

'I will make amends,' said the knight, 'unto my power.'

Sir Gawain would no mercy have but unlaced his helm to have stricken off his head. Right so came his lady out of a chamber and fell over him, and so he smote off her head by misadventure.

'Alas,' said Gaheris, 'that is foul and shamefully done, that shame shall never from you; also ye should give mercy unto them that ask mercy, for a knight without mercy is without worship.'

Sir Gawain was so stonied of the death of this fair lady that he wist not what he did, and said unto the knight, 'Arise, I will give thee mercy.'

'Nay, nay,' said the knight, 'I take no force of mercy now, for thou hast slain my love and my lady that I loved best of all earthly thing.'

'Me sore repenteth it,' said Sir Gawain, 'for I thought to strike unto thee. But now thou shalt go unto King Arthur and tell him of thine adventures, and how thou art overcome by the knight that went in the quest of the white hart.'

'I take no force,' said the knight, 'whether I live or I die;' but so for dread of death he swore to go unto King Arthur, and he made him to bear one greyhound before him on his horse, and another behind him.

'What is your name,' said Sir Gawain, 'or we depart?'

'My name is,' said the knight, 'Ablamor of the Marsh.'

So he departed toward Camelot.

[. . .]

Book VI

How Sir Launcelot and Sir Lionel departed from the
court for to seek adventures, and how Sir Lionel left
him sleeping and was taken

Soon after that King Arthur was come from Rome into England, then all the knights of the Table Round resorted unto the king, and made many jousts and tournaments. And some there were that were but knights, which increased so in arms and worship that they passed all their fellows in prowess and noble deeds, and that was well proved on many; but in especial it was proved on Sir Launcelot du Lake, for in all tournaments and jousts and deeds of arms, both for life and death, he passed all other knights, and at no time he was never overcome but if it were by treason or enchantment, so Sir Launcelot increased so he marvellously in worship, and in honour, therefore is he the first knight that the French book maketh mention of after King Arthur came from Rome. Wherefore Queen Guenever had him in great favour above all knights, and in certain he loved the queen again above all other ladies damosels of his life, and for her he did many deeds of arms, and saved her from the fire through his noble chivalry.

Thus Sir Launcelot rested him long with play and

game. And then he thought himself to prove himself in strange adventures, then he bad his nephew, Sir Lionel, for to make him ready, 'for we two will seek adventures.'

So they mounted on their horses, armed at all rights, and rode into a deep forest and so into a deep plain. And then the weather was hot about noon, and Sir Launcelot had great lust to sleep. Then Sir Lionel espied a great apple tree that stood by an hedge, and said, 'Brother, yonder is a fair shadow, there may we rest us on our horses.'

'It is well said, fair brother,' said Sir Launcelot, 'for this seven year I was not so sleepy as I am now.'

And so they there alighted and tied their horses unto sundry trees, and so Sir Launcelot laid him down under an apple tree, and his helm he laid under his head. And Sir Lionel waked while he slept. So Sir Launcelot was asleep passing fast.

And in the meanwhile there came three knights riding, as fast fleeing as ever they might ride. And there followed them three but one knight. And when Sir Lionel saw him, him thought he saw never so great a knight, nor so well faring a man, neither so well apparelled unto all rights.

So within a while this strong knight had overtaken one of these knights, and there he smote him to the cold earth that he lay still. And then he rode unto the second knight, and smote him so that man and horse fell down. And then straight to the third knight he rode, and smote him behind his horse's arse a spear length. And then he alit down and reined his horse on the bridle, and bound all the three knights fast with the reins of their own bridles.

When Sir Lionel saw him do thus, he thought to assay him, and made him ready, and stilly and privily he took his horse, and thought not for to awake Sir Launcelot. And when he was mounted upon his horse, he overtook this strong knight, and bad him turn, and the other smote Sir Lionel so hard that horse and man he bare to the earth, and so he alit down and bound him fast, and threw him overthwart his own horse, and so he served them all four, and rode with them away to his own castle.

And when he came there he gart unarm them, and beat them with thorns all naked, and after put them in a deep prison where were many more knights that made great dolour.

[. . .]

CHAPTER 3:
*How four queens found Launcelot sleeping, and
how by enchantment he was taken and led into
a castle*

Now leave we these knights prisoners, and speak we of Sir Launcelot du Lake that lieth under the apple tree sleeping. Even about the noon there come by him four queens of great estate; and, for the heat should not nigh them, there rode four knights about them, and bare a cloth of green silk on four spears, betwixt them and the sun, and the queens rode on four white mules.

Thus as they rode they heard by them a great horse grimly neigh, then were they ware of a sleeping knight, that lay all armed under an apple tree; anon as these queens looked on his face, they knew it was Sir Launcelot. Then they began for to strive for that knight, every each one said they would have him to her love.

'We shall not strive,' said Morgan le Fay, that was King Arthur's sister, 'I shall put an enchantment upon him that he shall not awake in six hours, and then I will lead him away unto my castle, and when he is surely within my hold, I shall take the enchantment from him, and then let him choose which of us he will have unto paramour.'

So this enchantment was cast upon Sir Launcelot, and then they laid him upon his shield, and bare him so on horseback betwixt two knights, and brought him unto the castle Chariot, and there they laid him in a chamber cold, and at night they sent unto him a fair damosel with his supper ready dight. By that the enchantment was past, and when she came she saluted him, and asked him what cheer.

'I cannot say, fair damosel,' said Sir Launcelot, 'for I wot not how I came into this castle but it be by an enchantment.'

'Sir,' said she, 'ye must make good cheer, and if ye be such a knight as it is said ye be, I shall tell you more to-morn by prime of the day.'

'Gramercy, fair damosel,' said Sir Launcelot, 'of your good will I require you.'

And so she departed. And there he lay all that night without comfort of anybody. And on the morn early came these four queens, passingly well beseen, all they bidding him good morn, and he them again.

'Sir knight,' the four queens said, 'thou must understand thou art our prisoner, and we here know thee well that thou art Sir Launcelot du Lake, King Ban's son, and because we understand your worthiness, that thou art the noblest knight living, and as we know well there can no lady have thy love but one, and that is Queen Guenever, and now thou shalt lose her for ever, and she thee, and therefore thee behoveth now to choose one of us four.'

'I am the Queen Morgan le Fay, queen of the land of Gore, and here is the Queen of Northgales, and the Queen of Eastland, and the Queen of the Out Isles; now choose one of us which thou wilt have to thy paramour, for thou mayest not choose or else in this prison to die.'

'This is an hard case,' said Sir Launcelot, 'that either I must die or else choose one of you, yet had I lever to die in this prison with worship, than to have one of you to my paramour maugre my head. And therefore ye be answered, I will none of you, for ye be false enchantresses, and as for my lady, Dame Guenever, were I at my liberty as I was, I would prove it on you or on yours, that she is the truest lady unto her lord living.'

'Well,' said the queens, 'is this your answer, that ye will refuse us?'

'Yea, on my life,' said Sir Launcelot, 'refused ye be of me.'

So they departed and left him there alone that made great sorrow.

CHAPTER 4:
How Sir Launcelot was delivered by the mean of a damosel

Right so at the noon came the damosel unto him with his dinner, and asked him what cheer.

'Truly, fair damosel,' said Sir Launcelot, 'in my life days never so ill.'

'Sir,' she said, 'that me repentest, but and ye will be ruled by me, I shall help you out of this distress, and ye shall have no shame nor villainy, so that ye hold me a promise.'

'Fair damosel, I will grant you, and sore I am of these queens sorceresses afeared, for they have destroyed many a good knight.'

'Sir,' said she, 'that is sooth, and for the renown and bounty that they hear of you they would have your love, and sir, they say, your name is Sir Launcelot du Lake, the flower of knights, and they be passing wroth with you that ye have refused them. But sir, and ye would promise me to help my father on Tuesday next coming, that hath made a tournament betwixt him and the King of Northgales, for the last Tuesday past my father lost the field through three knights of Arthur's court, and ye will be there on Tuesday next coming, and help my father, to-morn or prime, by the grace of God, I shall deliver you clean.'

'Fair maiden,' said Sir Launcelot, 'tell me what is your father's name, and then shall I give you an answer.'

'Sir knight,' she said, 'my father is King Bagdemagus, that was foul rebuked at the last tournament.'

'I know your father well,' said Sir Launcelot, 'for a noble king and a good knight, and by the faith of my body, ye shall have my body ready to do your father and you service at that day.'

'Sir,' she said, 'gramercy, and to-morn await ye be ready betimes, and I shall be she that shall deliver you, and take you your armour and your horse, shield and spear, and hereby, within this ten mile, is an abbey of white monks, there I pray you that ye me abide, and thither shall I bring my father unto you.'

'All this shall be done,' said Sir Launcelot, 'as I am true knight.'

And so she departed, and came on the morn early, and found him ready; then she brought him out of twelve locks, and brought him unto his armour, and when he was clean armed, she brought him until his own horse, and lightly he saddled him and took a great spear in his hand, and so rode forth, and said, 'Fair damosel, I shall not fail you by the grace of God.'

And so he rode into a great forest all that day, and never could find no highway, and so the night fell on him, and then was he ware in a slade, of a pavilion of red sendal.

'By my faith,' said Sir Launcelot, 'in that pavilion will I lodge all this night,' and so there he alit down, and tied his horse to the pavilion, and there he unarmed him, and there he found a bed, and laid him therein and fell asleep sadly.

CHAPTER 5:

How a knight found Sir Launcelot lying in his leman's bed, and how Sir Launcelot fought with the knight

Then within an hour there came the knight to whom the pavilion ought, and he weened that his leman had lain in that bed, and so he laid him down beside Sir Launcelot, and took him in his arms and began to kiss him.

And when Sir Launcelot felt a rough beard kissing him, he start out of the bed lightly, and the other knight after him, and either of them gat their swords in their hands, and out at the pavilion door went the knight of the pavilion, and Sir Launcelot followed him, and there by a little slake Sir Launcelot wounded him sore, nigh unto the death. And then he yielded him unto Sir Launcelot, and so he granted him, so that he would tell him why he came in to the bed.

'Sir,' said the knight, 'the pavilion is mine own, and there this night I had assigned my lady to have slept with me, and now I am likely to die of this wound.'

'That me repenteth,' said Launcelot, 'of your hurt, but I was adread of treason, for I was late beguiled, and therefore come on your way into your pavilion and take your rest, and as I suppose I shall staunch your blood.'

And so they went both into the pavilion, and anon Sir Launcelot staunched his blood. Therewithal came the knight's lady, that was a passing fair lady, and when she espied that her lord Belleus was sore wounded, she cried out on Sir Launcelot, and made great dole out of measure.

'Peace, my lady and my love,' said Belleus, 'for this knight is a good man, and a knight adventurous,' and there he told her all the cause how he was wounded; 'And when that I yielded me unto him, he left me goodly and hath staunched my blood.'

'Sir,' said the lady, 'I require thee tell me what knight ye be, and what is your name?'

'Fair lady,' he said, 'my name is Sir Launcelot du Lake.'

'So me thought ever by your speech,' said the lady, 'for I have seen you oft or this, and I know you better than ye ween. But now and ye would promise me of your courtesy, for the harms that ye have done to me and to my lord Belleus, that when he cometh unto Arthur's court for to cause him to be made knight of the Round Table, for he is a passing good man of arms, and a mighty lord of lands of many out isles.'

'Fair lady,' said Sir Launcelot, 'let him come unto the court the next high feast, and look that ye come with him, and I shall do my power, and ye prove you doughty of your hands, that ye shall have your desire.'

So thus within a while as they thus talked the night passed, and the day shone, and then Sir Launcelot armed him, and took his horse, and they taught him to the abbey, and thither he rode within the space of two hours.

[. . .]

How Sir Launcelot slew two giants, and made a castle free

Anon withal came there upon him two great giants, well armed all save the heads, with two horrible clubs in their hands. Sir Launcelot put his shield afore him and put the stroke away of the one giant, and with his sword he clave his head asunder. When his fellow saw that, he ran away as he were wood, for fear of the horrible strokes, and Launcelot after him with all his might, and smote him on the shoulder, and clave him to the navel.

Then Sir Launcelot went into the hall, and there came afore him three score ladies and damosels, and all kneeled unto him, and thanked God and him of their deliverance. 'For sir,' said they, 'the most part of us have been here this seven year their prisoners, and we have worked all manner of silk works for our meat, and we are all great gentlewomen born. And blessed be the time, knight, that ever thou be born; for thou hast done the most worship that ever did knight in this world, that will we bear record, and we all pray you to tell us your name, that we may tell our friends who delivered us out of prison.'

'Fair damosel,' he said, 'my name is Sir Launcelot du Lake.'

'Ah, sir,' said they all, 'well mayest thou be he, for else save yourself, as we deemed, there might never knight have the better of these two giants; for many fair knights have assayed it, and here have ended, and many times have we wished after you, and these two giants dread never knight but you.'

'Now may ye say,' said Sir Launcelot, 'unto your friends how and who hath delivered you, and greet them all from me, and if that I come in any of your marches, show me such cheer as ye have cause, and what treasure that there in this castle is I give it you for a reward for your grievance. And the lord that is owner of this castle I would he received it as is right.'

'Fair sir,' said they, 'the name of this castle is Tintagel, and a duke ought it sometime that had wedded fair Igraine and after wedded her Uther Pendragon, and gat on her Arthur.'

'Well,' said Sir Launcelot, 'I understand to whom this castle belongeth;' and so he departed from them, and betaught them unto God.

And then he mounted upon his horse, and rode into many strange and wild countries, and through many waters and valleys, and evil was he lodged. And at the last by fortune him happened, against a night, to come to a fair courtelage, and therein he found an old gentle-woman that lodged him with good will, and there he had good cheer for him and his horse. And when time was, his host brought him into a fair garret, over the gate, to his bed. There Sir Launcelot unarmed him, and set his harness by him, and went to bed, and anon he fell asleep.

So, soon after, there came one on horseback, and knocked at the gate in great haste, and when Sir Launcelot heard this, he arose up and looked out at the window, and saw by the moonlight three knights came riding after that one man, and all three lashed on him at once with swords, and that one knight turned on them knightly again, and defended him.

'Truly,' said Sir Launcelot, 'yonder one knight shall I help, for it were shame for me to see three knights on one. And if he be slain I am partner of his death,' and therewith he took his harness, and went out at a window by a sheet down to the four knights, and then Sir Launcelot said on high, 'Turn you knights unto me, and leave your fighting with that knight.'

And then they all three left Sir Kay, and turned unto Sir Launcelot, and there began great battle, for they alit all three, and struck many great strokes at Sir Launcelot, and assailed him on every side. Then Sir Kay dressed him for to have holpen Sir Launcelot.

'Nay, sir,' said he, 'I will none of your help; therefore as ye will have my help, let me alone with them.'

Sir Kay, for the pleasure of the knight, suffered him for to do his will, and so stood aside. And then anon within six strokes, Sir Launcelot had stricken them to the earth. And then they all three cried, 'Sir knight, we yield us unto you as man of might, makeless.'

'As to that,' said Sir Launcelot, 'I will not take your yielding unto me. But so that ye will yield you unto Sir Kay the Seneschal, on that covenant I will save your lives, and else not.'

'Fair knight,' said they, 'that were we loth to do; for as for Sir Kay, we chased him hither, and had overcome him had not ye been, therefore to yield us unto him it were no reason.'

'Well, as to that,' said Launcelot, 'advise you well, for ye may choose whether ye will die or live, for and ye be yielden it shall be unto Sir Kay.'

'Fair knight,' then they said, 'in saving of our lives we will do as thou commandest us.'

'Then shall ye,' said Sir Launcelot, 'on Whitsunday next coming, go unto the court of King Arthur and there shall ye yield you unto Queen Guenever, and put you all three in her grace and mercy, and say that Sir Kay sent you thither to be her prisoners.'

'Sir,' they said, 'it shall be done by the faith of our bodies, and we be living,' and there they swore every knight upon his sword.

And so Sir Launcelot suffered them so to depart. And then Sir Launcelot knocked at the gate with the pommel of his sword, and with that came his host, and in they entered Sir Kay and he.

'Sir,' said his host, 'I weened ye had been in your bed.'

'So I was,' said Sir Launcelot, 'but I arose and leapt out at my window for to help an old fellow of mine.'

And so when they came nigh the light, Sir Kay knew well that it was Sir Launcelot, and therewith he kneeled down and thanked him of all his kindness that he had holpen him twice from the death.

'Sir,' he said, 'I have nothing done but that me ought for to do, and ye are welcome, and here shall ye repose you and take your rest.'

So when Sir Kay was unarmed, he asked after meat; so there was meat fetched him, and he ate strongly. And when he had supped they went to their beds and were lodged together in one bed.

On the morn Sir Launcelot arose early, and left Sir Kay sleeping, and Sir Launcelot took Sir Kay's armour and his shield, and armed him, and so he went to the stable, and took his horse, and took his leave of his host, and so he departed. Then soon after arose Sir Kay and missed Sir Launcelot. And then he espied that he had his armour and his horse.

'Now by my faith I know well that he will grieve some of the court of King Arthur; for on him knights will be bold, and deem that it is I, and that will beguile them. And because of his armour and shield I am sure I shall ride in peace.'

And then soon after departed Sir Kay and thanked his host.

[. . .]

Book XI

How Sir Launcelot rode on his adventure, and how he helped a dolorous lady from her pain, and how that he fought with a dragon

Now leave we Sir Tristram de Liones, and speak we of Sir Launcelot du Lake, and of Sir Galahad, Sir Launcelot's son, how he was gotten, and in what manner, as the book of French rehearseth.

Afore the time that Sir Galahad was gotten or born, there came in an hermit unto King Arthur upon Whitsunday, as the knights sat at the Table Round. And when the hermit saw the Siege Perilous, he asked the king and all the knights why that siege was void.

Sir Arthur and all the knights answered, 'There shall never none sit in that siege but one, but if he be destroyed.'

Then said the hermit, 'Wot ye what is he?'

'Nay,' said Arthur and all the knights, 'we wot not who is he that shall sit therein.'

'Then wot I,' said the hermit, 'for he that shall sit there is unborn and ungotten, and this same year he shall be gotten that shall sit there in that Siege Perilous, and he shall win the Sangrail.' When this hermit had made this mention he departed from the court of King Arthur.

And then after this feast Sir Launcelot rode on his

adventure, till on a time by adventure he passed over the Pounte of Corbin; and there he saw the fairest tower that ever he saw, and thereunder was a fair town full of people; and all the people, men and women, cried at once, 'Welcome, Sir Launcelot du Lake, the flower of all knighthood, for by thee all we shall be holpen out of danger.'

'What mean ye,' said Sir Launcelot, 'that ye cry so upon me?'

'Ah, fair knight,' said they all, 'here is within this tower a dolorous lady that hath been there in pains many winters and days, for ever she boileth in scalding water; and but late,' said all the people, 'Sir Gawain was here and he might not help her, and so he left her in pain.'

'So may I,' said Sir Launcelot, 'leave her in pain as well as Sir Gawain did.'

'Nay,' said the people, 'we know well that it is Sir Launcelot that shall deliver her.'

'Well,' said Launcelot, 'then show me what I shall do.'

Then they brought Sir Launcelot into the tower; and when he came to the chamber thereas this lady was, the doors of iron unlocked and unbolted. And so Sir Launcelot went into the chamber that was as hot as any stew. And there Sir Launcelot took the fairest lady by the hand that ever he saw, and she was naked as a needle; and by enchantment Queen Morgan le Fay and the Queen of Northgales had put her there in that pains, because she was called the fairest lady of that country; and there she had been five years, and never might she be delivered out of her great pains unto the time the best knight of the world had taken her by the hand.

Then the people brought her clothes. And when she was arrayed, Sir Launcelot thought she was the fairest lady of the world, but if it were Queen Guenever.

Then this lady said to Sir Launcelot, 'Sir, if it please you will ye go with me hereby into a chapel that we may give loving and thanking unto God?'

'Madam,' said Sir Launcelot, 'cometh on with me, I will go with you.'

So when they came there and gave thankings to God all the people, both learned and lewd, gave thankings unto God and him, and said, 'Sir knight, since ye have delivered this lady, ye shall deliver us from a serpent that is here in a tomb.'

Then Sir Launcelot took his shield and said, 'Bring me thither, and what I may do unto the pleasure of God and you I will do.'

So when Sir Launcelot came thither he saw written upon the tomb letters of gold that said thus: HERE SHALL COME A LEOPARD OF KINGS' BLOOD, AND HE SHALL SLAY THIS SERPENT, AND THIS LEOPARD SHALL ENGENDER A LION IN THIS FOREIGN COUNTRY, THE WHICH LION SHALL PASS ALL OTHER KNIGHTS.

So then Sir Launcelot lift up the tomb, and there came out an horrible and a fiendly dragon, spitting fire out of his mouth. Then Sir Launcelot drew his sword and fought with the dragon long, and at the last with great pain Sir Launcelot slew that dragon.

Therewithal came King Pelles, the good and noble knight, and saluted Sir Launcelot, and he him again.

'Fair knight,' said the king, 'what is your name? I require you of your knighthood tell me!'

CHAPTER 2:
How Sir Launcelot came to Pelles, and of the Sangrail, and how he begat Galahad on Elaine, King Pelles' daughter

'Sir,' said Launcelot, 'wit you well my name is Sir Launcelot du Lake.'

'And my name is,' said the king, 'Pelles, king of the foreign country, and cousin nigh unto Joseph of Arimathea.'

And then either of them made much of other, and so they went into the castle to take their repast. And anon there came in a dove at a window, and in her mouth there seemed a little censer of gold. And therewithal there was such a savour as all the spicery of the world had been there. And forthwithal there was upon the table all manner of meats and drinks that they could think upon.

So came in a damosel passing fair and young, and she bare a vessel of gold betwixt her hands; and thereto the king kneeled devoutly, and said his prayers, and so did all that were there.

'O Jesu!' said Sir Launcelot, 'What may this mean?'

'This is,' said the king, 'the richest thing that any man hath living. And when this thing goeth about, the Round Table shall be broken; and wit thou well,' said the king, 'this is the holy Sangrail that ye have here seen.'

So the king and Sir Launcelot led their life the most part of that day. And fain would King Pelles have found the mean to have had Sir Launcelot to have lain by his daughter, fair Elaine. And for this intent: the king knew well that Sir Launcelot should get a child upon his daughter, the which should be named Sir Galahad, the good knight, by whom all the foreign country should be brought out of danger, and by him the Holy Grail should be achieved.

Then came forth a lady that hight Dame Brisen, and she said unto the king, 'Sir, wit ye well Sir Launcelot loveth no lady in the world but all only Queen Guenever; and therefore work ye by counsel, and I shall make him to lie with your daughter, and he shall not wit but that he lieth with Queen Guenever.'

'O fair lady, Dame Brisen,' said the king, 'hope ye to bring this about?'

'Sir,' said she, 'upon pain of my life let me deal;' for this Brisen was one of the greatest enchantresses that was at that time in the world living.

Then anon by Dame Brisen's wit she made one to come to Sir Launcelot that he knew well. And this man brought him a ring from Queen Guenever like as it had come from her, and such one as she was wont for the most part to wear; and when Sir Launcelot saw that token wit ye well he was never so fain.

'Where is my lady?' said Sir Launcelot.

'In the Castle of Case,' said the messenger, 'but five mile thence.'

Then Sir Launcelot thought to be there the same night. And then this Brisen by the commandment of King Pelles let send Elaine to this castle with twenty-five knights unto the Castle of Case. Then Sir Launcelot against night rode unto that castle, and there anon he was received worshipfully with such people to his seeming as were about Queen Guenever secret. So when Sir Launcelot was alit, he asked where the queen was. So Dame Brisen said she was in her bed; and then the people were avoided, and Sir Launcelot was led unto his chamber.

And then Dame Brisen brought Sir Launcelot a cupful of wine; and anon as he had drunken that wine he was so assotted and mad that he might make no delay, but withouten any let he went to bed; and he weened that maiden Elaine had been Queen Guenever. Wit you well that Sir Launcelot was glad, and so was that lady Elaine that she had gotten Sir Launcelot in her arms. For well she knew that same night should be gotten upon her Galahad that should prove the best knight of the world; and so they lay together until undern on the morn; and all the windows and holes of that chamber were stopped that no manner of day might be seen.

And then Sir Launcelot remembered him, and he arose up and went to the window.

CHAPTER 3:

How Sir Launcelot was displeased when he knew that he had lain by Elaine, and how she was delivered of Galahad

And anon as he had unshut the window the enchantment was gone; then he knew himself that he had done amiss.

'Alas,' he said, 'that I have lived so long; now I am shamed.'

So then he gat his sword in his hand and said, 'Thou traitoress, what art thou that I have lain by all this night? Thou shalt die right here of my hands.'

Then this fair lady Elaine skipped out of her bed all naked, and kneeled down afore Sir Launcelot, and said, 'Fair courteous knight, comen of kings' blood, I require you have mercy upon me, and as thou art renowned the most noble knight of the world, slay me not, for I have in my womb him by thee that shall be the most noblest knight of the world.'

'Ah, false traitoress,' said Sir Launcelot, 'why hast thou betrayed me? Anon tell me what thou art.'

'Sir,' she said, 'I am Elaine, the daughter of King Pelles.'

'Well,' said Sir Launcelot, 'I will forgive you this deed;' and therewith he took her up in his arms, and kissed her, for she was as fair a lady, and thereto lusty and young, and as wise, as any was that time living. 'So God me help,' said Sir Launcelot, 'I may not wit this to you; but her that made this enchantment upon me as between you and me, and I may find her, that same Lady Brisen, she shall lose her head for witchcrafts, for there was never knight deceived so as I am this night.'

And so Sir Launcelot arrayed him, and armed him, and took his leave mildly at that lady young Elaine, and so he departed.

Then she said, 'My lord Sir Launcelot, I beseech you see me as soon as ye may, for I have obeyed me unto the prophecy that my father told me. And by his commandment to fulfil this prophecy I have given the greatest riches and the fairest flower that ever I had, and that is my maidenhood that I shall never have again; and therefore, gentle knight, owe me your goodwill.'

And so Sir Launcelot arrayed him and was armed, and took his leave mildly at that young lady Elaine; and so he departed, and rode till he came to the Castle of Corbin, where her father was.

And as fast as her time came she was delivered of a fair child, and they christened him Galahad; and wit ye well that child was well kept and well nourished, and he was named Galahad because Sir Launcelot was so named at the fountain stone; and after that, the Lady of the Lake confirmed him Sir Launcelot du Lake.

Then after this lady was delivered and churched there came a knight unto her, his name was Sir Bromel la Pleche, the which was a great lord; and he had loved that lady long, and he evermore desired her to wed her; and so by no mean she could put him off, till on a day she said to Sir Bromel,

'Wit thou well, sir knight, I will not love you, for my love is set upon the best knight of the world.'

'Who is he?' said Sir Bromel.

'Sir,' she said, 'it is Sir Launcelot du Lake that I love and none other, and therefore woo me no longer.'

'Ye say well,' said Sir Bromel, 'and sithen ye have told me so much, ye shall have but little joy of Sir Launcelot, for I shall slay him wheresomever I meet him.'

'Sir,' said the Lady Elaine, 'do to him no treason.'

'Wit ye well, my lady,' said Bromel, 'and I promise you this twelvemonth I shall keep the Pounte of Corbin for Sir Launcelot's sake, that he shall neither come ne go unto you, but I shall meet with him.'

CHAPTER 4:
How Sir Bors came to Dame Elaine and saw
Galahad, and how he was fed with the Sangrail

Then as it fell by fortune and adventure, Sir Bors de
Ganis, that was nephew unto Sir Launcelot, came over
that bridge; and there Sir Bromel and Sir Bors jousted,
and Sir Bors smote Sir Bromel such a buffet that he bare
him over his horse's croup.

And then Sir Bromel as an hardy knight pulled out
his sword, and dressed his shield to do battle with Sir
Bors. And then Sir Bors alit and avoided his horse, and
there they dashed together many sad strokes; and long
thus they fought, till at the last Sir Bromel was laid to
the earth, and there Sir Bors began to unlace his helm to
slay him. Then Sir Bromel cried Sir Bors mercy, and
yielded him.

'Upon this covenant thou shalt have thy life,' said Sir
Bors, 'so thou go unto Sir Launcelot upon Whitsunday
that next cometh, and yield thee unto him as knight
recreant.'

'I will do it,' said Sir Bromel, and that he sware upon
the cross of the sword.

And so he let him depart, and Sir Bors rode unto King
Pelles, that was within Corbin. And when the king and
Elaine his daughter wist that Sir Bors was nephew unto
Sir Launcelot, they made him great cheer.

Then said Dame Elaine, 'We marvel where Sir
Launcelot is, for he came never here but once.'

'Marvel not,' said Sir Bors, 'for this half year he hath

been in prison with Queen Morgan le Fay, King Arthur's sister.'

'Alas,' said Dame Elaine, 'that me repenteth.'

And ever Sir Bors beheld that child in her arms, and ever him seemed it was passing like Sir Launcelot.

'Truly,' said Elaine, 'wit ye well this child he gat upon me.'

Then Sir Bors wept for joy, and he prayed to God it might prove as good a knight as his father was.

And so came in a white dove, and she bare a little censer of gold in her mouth, and there was all manner of meats and drinks; and a maiden bare that Sangrail, and she said openly, 'Wit you well, Sir Bors, that this child is Galahad, that shall sit in the Siege Perilous, and achieve the Sangrail, and he shall be much better than ever was Sir Launcelot du Lake, that is his own father.'

And then they kneeled down and made their devotions, and there was such a savour as all the spicery in the world had been there. And when the dove took her flight, the maiden vanished with the Sangrail as she came.

'Sir,' said Sir Bors unto King Pelles, 'this castle may be named the Castle Adventurous, for here be many strange adventures.'

'That is sooth,' said the king, 'for well may this place be called the adventurous place, for there come but few knights here that go away with any worship; be he never so strong, here he may be proved; and but late Sir Gawain, the good knight, gat but little worship here. For I let you wit,' said King Pelles, 'here shall no knight win no worship but if he be of worship himself and of good living, and that loveth God and dreadeth God, and else he getteth no worship here, be he never so hardy.'

'That is wonderful thing,' said Sir Bors. 'What ye mean in this country I wot not, for ye have many strange adventures, and therefore I will lie in this castle this night.'

'Ye shall not do so,' said King Pelles, 'by my counsel, for it is hard and ye escape without a shame.'

'I shall take the adventure that will befall me,' said Sir Bors.

'Then I counsel you,' said the king, 'to be confessed clean.'

'As for that,' said Sir Bors, 'I will be shriven with a good will.'

So Sir Bors was confessed, and for all women Sir Bors was a virgin, save for one, that was the daughter of King Brandegoris, and on her he gat a child that hight Helin, and save for her Sir Bors was a clean maiden.

And so Sir Bors was led unto bed in a fair large chamber, and many doors were shut about the chamber. When Sir Bors espied all those doors, he avoided all the people, for he might have nobody with him; but in no wise Sir Bors would unarm him, but so he laid him down upon the bed.

And right so he saw come in a light, that he might well see a spear great and long that came straight upon him pointling, and to Sir Bors seemed that the head of the spear burnt like a taper. And anon or Sir Bors wist, the spear head smote him into the shoulder an handbreath in deepness, and that wound grieved Sir Bors passing sore.

And then he laid him down again for pain; and anon

therewithal there came a knight armed with his shield on his shoulder and his sword in his hand, and he bad Sir Bors: 'Arise, sir knight, and fight with me.'

'I am sore hurt,' he said, 'but yet I shall not fail thee.'

And then Sir Bors start up and dressed his shield; and then they lashed together mightily a great while; and at the last Sir Bors bare him backward until that he came unto a chamber door, and there that knight yede into that chamber and rested him a great while. And when he had reposed him he came out freshly again, and began new battle with Sir Bors mightily and strongly.

CHAPTER 5:

How Sir Bors made Sir Pedivere to yield him, and of marvellous adventures that he had, and how he achieved them

Then Sir Bors thought he should no more go into that chamber to rest him, and so Sir Bors dressed him betwixt the knight and that chamber door, and there Sir Bors smote him down, and then that knight yielded him.

'What is your name?' said Sir Bors.

'Sir,' said he, 'my name is Pedivere of the Strait Marches.'

So Sir Bors made him to swear at Whitsunday next coming to be at the court of King Arthur, and yield him there as a prisoner as an overcome knight by the hands of Sir Bors. So thus departed Sir Pedivere of the Strait Marches.

And then Sir Bors laid him down to rest, and then he

heard and felt much noise in that chamber, and then Sir Bors espied that there came in, he wist not whether at the doors nor windows, shot of arrows and of quarrels so thick that he marvelled, and many fell upon him and hurt him in the bare places.

And then Sir Bors was ware where came in an hideous lion; so Sir Bors dressed him unto the lion, and anon the lion bereft him his shield, and with his sword Sir Bors smote off the lion's head.

Right so Sir Bors forthwithal saw a dragon in the court passing horrible, and there seemed letters of gold written in his forehead; and Sir Bors thought that the letters made a signification of King Arthur.

Right so there came an horrible leopard and an old, and there they fought long, and did great battle together. And at the last the dragon spit out of his mouth as it had been an hundred dragons; and lightly all the small dragons slew the old dragon and tare him all to pieces.

Anon withal there came an old man into the hall, and he sat him down in a fair chair, and there seemed to be two adders about his neck; and then the old man had an harp, and there he sang an old song how Joseph of Arimathea came into this land. Then when he had sungen, the old man bad Sir Bors go from thence.

'For here shall ye have no more adventures; and full worshipfully have ye done, and better shall ye do hereafter.'

And then Sir Bors seemed that there came the whitest dove with a little golden censer in her mouth. And anon therewithal the tempest ceased and passed, that afore was marvellous to hear. So was all that court full of good savours. Then Sir Bors saw four children bearing four fair tapers, and an old man in the midst of the children with a censer in his one hand, and a spear in his other hand, and that spear was called the spear of vengeance.

CHAPTER 6:

How Sir Bors departed; and how Sir Launcelot was rebuked of the queen Guenever, and of his excuse

'Now,' said that old man to Sir Bors, 'go ye to your cousin, Sir Launcelot, and tell him of this adventure the which had been most convenient for him of all earthly knights; but sin is so foul in him he may not achieve such holy deeds, for had not been his sin he had passed all the knights that ever were in his days; and tell thou Sir Launcelot, of all worldly adventures he passeth in manhood and prowess all other, but in these spiritual matters he shall have many his better.'

And then Sir Bors saw four gentlewomen come by him, poorly beseen; and he saw where that they entered into a chamber where was great light as it were a summer light; and the women kneeled down afore an altar of silver with four pillars, and as it had been a bishop kneeled down afore that table of silver. And as Sir Bors looked over his head he saw a sword like silver naked hoving over his head, and the clearnes thereof smote so in his eyen that as at that time Sir Bors was blind; and there he heard a voice that said, 'Go hence, thou Sir Bors, for as yet thou art not worthy for to be in this place.'

And then he yede backward to his bed till on the morn.

And on the morn King Pelles made great joy of Sir Bors; and then he departed and rode to Camelot, and there he found Sir Launcelot du Lake, and told him of the adventures that he had seen with King Pelles at Corbin.

So the noise sprang in Arthur's court that Launcelot had gotten a child upon Elaine, the daughter of King Pelles, wherefore Queen Guenever was wroth, and gave many rebukes to Sir Launcelot, and called him false knight. And then Sir Launcelot told the queen all, and how he was made to lie by her by enchantment in likeness of the queen. So the queen held Sir Launcelot excused.

And as the book saith, King Arthur had been in France, and had made war upon the mighty king Claudas, and had won much of his lands. And when the king was come again he let cry a great feast, that all lords and ladies of all England should be there, but if it were such as were rebellious against him.

CHAPTER 7:
How Dame Elaine, Galahad's mother, came in
great estate to Camelot, and how Launcelot behaved
him there

And when Dame Elaine, the daughter of King Pelles, heard of this feast she went to her father and required him that he would give her leave to ride to that feast.

The king answered, 'I will well ye go thither, but in

any wise as ye love me and will have my blessing, that ye be well beseen in the richest wise; and look that ye spare not for no cost; ask and ye shall have all that you needeth.'

Then by the advice of Dame Brisen, her maiden, all thing was apparelled unto the purpose, that there was never no lady more richlier beseen. So she rode with twenty knights, and ten ladies, and gentlewomen, to the number of an hundred horses. And when she came to Camelot, King Arthur and Queen Guenever said, and all the knights, that Dame Elaine was the fairest and the best beseen lady that ever was seen in that court.

And anon as King Arthur wist that she was come he met her and saluted her, and so did the most part of all the knights of the Round Table, both Sir Tristram, Sir Bleoberis, and Sir Gawain, and many more that I will not rehearse.

But when Sir Launcelot saw her he was so ashamed, and that because he drew his sword on the morn when he had lain by her, that he would not salute her nor speak to her; and yet Sir Launcelot thought she was the fairest woman that ever he saw in his life days.

But when Dame Elaine saw Sir Launcelot that would not speak unto her she was so heavy that she weened her heart would have to-brast, for wit you well, out of measure she loved him.

And then Elaine said unto her woman, Dame Brisen, 'The unkindness of Sir Launcelot slayeth me near.'

'Ah, peace, madam,' said Dame Brisen, 'I will undertake that this night shall he lie with you, and ye would hold you still.'

'That were me lever,' said Dame Elaine, 'than all the gold that is above the earth.'

'Let me deal,' said Dame Brisen.

So when Elaine was brought unto Queen Guenever either made other good cheer by countenance, but nothing with hearts. But all men and women spake of the beauty of Dame Elaine, and of her great riches.

Then at night the queen commanded that Dame Elaine should sleep in a chamber nigh her chamber, and all under one roof; and so it was done as the queen commanded. Then the queen sent for Sir Launcelot and bad him come to her chamber that night: 'Or else I am sure,' said the queen, 'that ye will go to your lady's bed, Dame Elaine, by whom ye gat Galahad.'

'Ah, madam,' said Sir Launcelot, 'never say ye so, for that I did was against my will.'

'Then,' said the queen, 'look that ye come to me when I send for you.'

'Madam,' said Launcelot, 'I shall not fail you, but I shall be ready at your commandment.'

This bargain was soon done and made between them, but Dame Brisen knew it by her crafts, and told it to her lady, Dame Elaine.

'Alas,' said she, 'how shall I do?'

'Let me deal,' said Dame Brisen, 'for I shall bring him by the hand even to your bed, and he shall ween that I am Queen Guenever's messenger.'

'Now well is me,' said Dame Elaine, 'for all the world I love not so much as I do Sir Launcelot.'

CHAPTER 8:
How Dame Brisen by enchantment brought Sir Launcelot to Dame Elaine's bed, and how Queen Guenever rebuked him

So when time came that all folks were abed, Dame Brisen came to Sir Launcelot's bed's side and said, 'Sir Launcelot du Lake, sleep you? My lady, Queen Guenever, lieth and awaiteth upon you.'

'O my fair lady,' said Sir Launcelot, 'I am ready to go with you where ye will have me.'

So Sir Launcelot threw upon him a long gown, and his sword in his hand; and then Dame Brisen took him by the finger and led him to her lady's bed, Dame Elaine; and then she departed and left them in bed together. Wit you well the lady was glad, and so was Sir Launcelot, for he weened that he had had another in his arms.

Now leave we them kissing and clipping, as was kindly thing; and now speak we of Queen Guenever that sent one of her women unto Sir Launcelot's bed; and when she came there she found the bed cold, and he was away; so she came to the queen and told her all.

'Alas,' said the queen, 'where is that false knight become?'

Then the queen was nigh out of her wit, and then she writhed and weltered as a mad woman, and might not sleep a four or five hours. Then Sir Launcelot had a condition that he used of custom, he would clatter in his sleep, and speak oft of his lady, Queen Guenever. So as Sir Launcelot had waked as long as it had pleased him, then by course of kind he slept, and Dame Elaine both. And in his sleep he talked and clattered as a jay, of the love that had been betwixt Queen Guenever and him. And so as he talked so loud the queen heard him there as she lay in her chamber; and when she heard him so clatter she was nigh wood and out of her mind, and for anger and pain wist not what to do. And then she coughed so loud that Sir Launcelot awaked, and he knew her heming. And then he knew well that he lay not by the queen; and therewith he leapt out of his bed as he had been a wood man, in his shirt, and the queen met him in the floor; and thus she said:

'False traitor knight that thou art, look thou never abide in my court, and avoid my chamber, and not so hardy, thou false traitor knight that thou art, that ever thou come in my sight!'

'Alas,' said Sir Launcelot; and therewith he took such an heartly sorrow at her words that he fell down to the floor in a swoon. And therewithal Queen Guenever departed.

And when Sir Launcelot awoke of his swoon, he leapt out at a bay window into a garden, and there with thorns he was all to-cratched in his visage and his body; and so he ran forth he wist not whither, and was wild wood as ever was man; and so he ran two year, and never man might have grace to know him.

CHAPTER 9:
How Dame Elaine was commanded by Queen Guenever to avoid the court, and how Sir Launcelot became mad

Now turn we unto Queen Guenever and to the fair Lady Elaine, that when Dame Elaine heard the queen so to rebuke Sir Launcelot, and also she saw how he swooned, and how he leapt out at a bay window, then she said unto Queen Guenever, 'Madam, ye are greatly to blame for Sir Launcelot, for now have ye lost him, for I saw and heard by his countenance that he is mad for ever. Alas, madam, ye do great sin, and to yourself great dishonour, for ye have a lord of your own, and therefore it is your part to love him; for there is no queen in this world hath such another king as ye have. And if ye were not I might have the love of my lord Sir Launcelot; and cause I have to love him for he had my maidenhood, and by him I have borne a fair son, and his name is Galahad, and he shall be in his time the best knight of the world.'

'Dame Elaine,' said the queen, 'when it is daylight I charge you and command you to avoid my court; and for the love ye owe unto Sir Launcelot discover not his counsel, for and ye do, it will be his death.'

'As for that,' said Dame Elaine, 'I dare undertake he is marred for ever, and that have ye made; for ye nor I are like to rejoice him, for he made the most piteous groans when he leapt out at yonder bay window that ever I heard man make. Alas,' said fair Elaine, and 'Alas,' said the Queen Guenever, 'for now I wot well we have lost him for ever.'

So on the morn Dame Elaine took her leave to depart, and she would no longer abide. Then King Arthur brought her on her way with more than an hundred knights through a forest. And by the way she told Sir Bors de Ganis all how it betid that same night, and how Sir Launcelot leapt out at a window araged out of his wit.

'Alas,' said Sir Bors, 'Where is my lord, Sir Launcelot, become?'

'Sir,' said Elaine, 'I wot nere.'

'Alas,' said Sir Bors, 'betwixt you both ye have destroyed that good knight.'

'As for me,' said Dame Elaine, 'I said never nor did never thing that should in any wise displease him, but with the rebuke that Queen Guenever gave him I saw him swoon to the earth; and when he awoke he took his sword in his hand, naked save his shirt, and leapt out at a window with the grisliest groan that ever I heard man make.'

'Now farewell, Dame Elaine,' said Sir Bors, 'and hold my lord Arthur with a tale as long as ye can, for I will turn again to Queen Guenever and give her a hete; and I require you, as ever ye will have my service, make good watch and espy if ever ye may see my lord Sir Launcelot.'

'Truly,' said fair Elaine, 'I shall do all that I may do, for as fain would I know and wit where he is become, as you, or any of his kin, or Queen Guenever; and cause great enough have I thereto as well as any other. And wit ye well,' said fair Elaine to Sir Bors, 'I would lose my life for him rather than he should be hurt; but alas, I cast me never for to see him, and the chief causer of this is Dame Guenever.'

'Madam,' said Dame Brisen, the which had made the enchantment before betwixt Sir Launcelot and her, 'I pray you heartily, let Sir Bors depart, and hie him with all his might as fast as he may to seek Sir Launcelot, for I warn you he is clean out of his mind; and yet he shall be well holpen and but by miracle.'

Then wept Dame Elaine, and so did Sir Bors de Ganis; and so they departed, and Sir Bors rode straight unto Queen Guenever. And when she saw Sir Bors she wept as she were wood.

'Fie on your weeping,' said Sir Bors de Ganis, 'for ye weep never but when there is no boot. Alas,' said Sir Bors, 'that ever Sir Launcelot's kin saw you, for now have ye lost the best knight of our blood, and he that was all our leader and our succour; and I dare say and make it good that all kings, Christian nor heathen, may not find such a knight, for to speak of his nobleness and courtesy, with his beauty and his gentleness. Alas,' said Sir Bors, 'what shall we do that be of his blood?'

'Alas,' said Ector de Maris.

'Alas,' said Lionel.

CHAPTER 10:

What sorrow Queen Guenever made for Sir Launcelot, and how he was sought by knights of his kin

And when the queen heard them say so she fell to the earth in a dead swoon. And then Sir Bors took her up, and dawed her; and when she was awaked she kneeled afore the three knights, and held up both their hands, and besought them to seek him. 'And spare not for no goods but that he be founden, for I wot he is out of his mind.'

And Sir Bors, Sir Ector, and Sir Lionel departed from the queen, for they might not abide no longer for sorrow. And then the queen sent them treasure enough for their expenses, and so they took their horses and their armour, and departed. And then they rode from country to country, in forests, and in wilderness, and in wastes; and ever they laid watch both at forests and at all manner of men as they rode, to hearken and spere after him, as he that was a naked man, in his shirt, with a sword in his hand.

And thus they rode nigh a quarter of a year, endlong and overthwart, in many places, forests and wilderness, and ofttimes were evil lodged for his sake; and yet for all their labour and seeking could they never hear word of him. And wit you well these three knights were passing sorry. Then at the last Sir Bors and his fellows met with a knight that hight Sir Melion de Tartare.

'Now fair knight,' said Sir Bors, 'whither be ye away?' For they knew either other afore time.

'Sir,' said Melion, 'I am in the way toward the court of King Arthur.'

'Then we pray you,' said Sir Bors, 'that ye will tell my lord Arthur, and my lady, Queen Guenever, and all the fellowship of the Round Table, that we cannot in no wise hear tell where Sir Launcelot is become.'

Then Sir Melion departed from them, and said that

he would tell the king, and the queen, and all the fellow-ship of the Round Table, as they had desired him. So when Sir Melion came to the court of King Arthur he told the king, and the queen, and all the fellowship of the Round Table, what Sir Bors had said of Sir Launcelot.

Then Sir Gawain, Sir Uwain, Sir Sagramore le Desirous, Sir Agloval, and Sir Percival de Gales took upon them by the great desire of King Arthur, and in especial by the queen, to seek throughout all England, Wales, and Scotland, to find Sir Launcelot, and with them rode eighteen knights more to bear them fellowship; and wit ye well, they lacked no manner of spending; and so were they three and twenty knights.

Now turn we to Sir Launcelot, and speak we of his care and woe, and what pain he there endured; for cold, hunger, and thirst, he had plenty.

And thus as these noble knights rode together, they by one assent departed, and then they rode by two, by three, and by four, and by five, and ever they assigned where they should meet. And so Sir Agloval and Sir Percival rode together unto their mother that was a queen in those days. And when she saw her two sons, for joy she wept tenderly. And then she said,

'Ah, my dear sons, when your father was slain he left me four sons, of the which now be twain slain. And for the death of my noble son, Sir Lamorak, shall my heart never be glad.'

And then she kneeled down upon her knees tofore Agloval and Sir Percival, and besought them to abide at home with her.

'Ah, sweet mother,' said Sir Percival, 'we may not, for

we come of kings' blood of both parties, and therefore, mother it is our kind to haunt arms and noble deeds.'

'Alas my sweet sons,' then she said, 'for your sakes I shall lose my liking and lust, and then wind and weather I may not endure, what for the death of your father, King Pellinor, that was shamefully slain by the hands of Sir Gawain, and his brother, Sir Gaheris: and they slew him not manly but by treason. Ah, my dear sons, this is a piteous complaint for me of your father's death, considering also the death of Sir Lamorak, that of knighthood had but few fellows. Now, my dear sons, have this in your mind.'

Then there was but weeping and sobbing in the court when they should depart, and she fell in swooning in midst of the court.

[. . .]

Book XXI

How Sir Mordred presumed and took on him to be king of England, and would have married the queen, his father's wife

As Sir Mordred was ruler of all England, he did do make letters as though that they came from beyond the sea, and the letters specified that King Arthur was slain in battle with Sir Launcelot. Wherefore Sir Mordred made a parliament, and called the lords together, and there he made them to choose him king; and so was he crowned at Canterbury, and held a feast there fifteen days; and afterward he drew him unto Winchester, and there he took the queen Guenever, and said plainly that he would wed her which was his uncle's wife and his father's wife. And so he made ready for the feast, and a day prefixed that they should be wedded; wherefore Queen Guenever was passing heavy. But she durst not discover her heart, but spake fair, and agreed to Sir Mordred's will.

Then she desired of Sir Mordred for to go to London, to buy all manner of things that longed unto the wedding. And because of her fair speech Sir Mordred trusted her well enough, and gave her leave to go. And so when she came to London she took the Tower of London, and suddenly in all haste possible she stuffed it with all manner of victual, and well garnished it with men, and so kept it.

Then when Sir Mordred wist and understood how he was beguiled, he was passing wroth out of measure. And a short tale for to make, he went and laid a mighty siege about the Tower of London, and made many great assaults thereat, and threw many great engines unto them, and shot great guns. But all might not prevail Sir Mordred, for Queen Guenever would never for fair speech nor for foul, would never trust to come in his hands again.

Then came the Bishop of Canterbury, the which was a noble clerk and an holy man, and thus he said to Sir Mordred: 'Sir, what will do? Will ye first displease God and sithen shame yourself, and all knighthood? Is not King Arthur your uncle, no farther but your mother's brother, and on her himself King Arthur begat you, upon his own sister, therefore how may you wed your father's wife? Sir,' said the noble clerk, 'leave this opinion or I shall curse you with book and bell and candle.'

'Do thou thy worst,' said Sir Mordred, 'wit thou well I shall defy thee.'

'Sir,' said the Bishop, 'and wit you well I shall not fear me to do that me ought to do. Also where ye noise where my lord Arthur is slain, and that is not so, and therefore ye will make a foul work in this land.'

'Peace, thou false priest,' said Sir Mordred, 'for and thou chafe me any more I shall make strike off thy head.'

So the Bishop departed and did the cursing in the most orgulest wise that might be done. And then Sir Mordred sought the Bishop of Canterbury, for to have slain him.

Then the Bishop fled, and took part of his goods with him, and went nigh unto Glastonbury; and there he was as priest hermit in a chapel, and lived in poverty and in holy prayers, for well he understood that mischievous war was at hand.

Then Sir Mordred sought on Queen Guenever by letters and sondes, and by fair means and foul means, for to have her to come out of the Tower of London; but all this availed not, for she answered him shortly, openly and privily, that she had lever slay herself than to be married with him.

Then came word to Sir Mordred that King Arthur had araised the siege for Sir Launcelot, and he was coming homeward with a great host, to be avenged upon Sir Mordred; wherefore Sir Mordred made write writs to all the barony of this land, and much people drew to him. For then was the common voice among them that with Arthur was none other life but war and strife, and with Sir Mordred was great joy and bliss. Thus was Sir Arthur depraved, and evil said of. And many there were that King Arthur had made up of nought, and given them lands, might not then say him a good word.

Lo ye all Englishmen, see ye not what a mischief here was? For he that was the most king and knight of the world, and most loved the fellowship of noble knights, and by him they were all upholden, now might not these Englishmen hold them content with him. Lo thus was the old custom and usage of this land; and also men say that we of this land have not yet lost ne forgotten that custom and usage. Alas, this is a great default of us Englishmen, for there may nothing please us no term.

And so fared the people at that time, they were better pleased with Sir Mordred than they were with King Arthur; and much people drew unto Sir Mordred, and said they would abide with him for better and for worse. And so Sir Mordred drew with a great host to Dover, for there he heard say that Sir Arthur would arrive, and so he thought to beat his own father from his lands; and the most part of all England held with Sir Mordred, the people were so new fangle.

CHAPTER 2:

How after that King Arthur had tidings, he returned and came to Dover, where Sir Mordred met him to let his landing; and of the death of Sir Gawain

And so as Sir Mordred was at Dover with his host, there came King Arthur with a great navy of ships, and galleys, and carracks. And there was Sir Mordred ready awaiting upon his landage, to let his own father to land up the land that he was king over.

Then there was launching of great boats and small, and full of noble men of arms; and there was much slaughter of gentle knights, and many a full bold baron was laid full low, on both parties.

But King Arthur was so courageous that there might no manner of knights let him to land, and his knights fiercely followed him; and so they landed maugre Sir Mordred's and all his power, and put Sir Mordred aback, that he fled and all his people.

So when this battle was done, King Arthur let bury his people that were dead. And then was noble Sir Gawain found in a great boat, lying more than half dead. When Sir Arthur wist that Sir Gawain was laid so low, he went unto him; and there the king made sorrow out of measure, and took Sir Gawain in his arms, and thrice he there swooned.

And then when he awaked, he said, 'Alas, Sir Gawain, my sister's son, here now thou liest, the man in the world that I loved most; and now is my joy gone, for now, my nephew Sir Gawain, I will discover me unto your person: in Sir Launcelot and you I most had my joy, and mine affiance, and now have I lost my joy of you both; wherefore all mine earthly joy is gone from me.'

'Mine uncle King Arthur,' said Sir Gawain, 'wit you well my death day is come, and all is through mine own hastiness and wilfulness; for I am smitten upon the old wound the which Sir Launcelot gave me, on the which I feel well I must die; and had Sir Launcelot been with you as he was, this unhappy war had never begun; and of all this am I causer, for Sir Launcelot and his blood, through their prowess, held all your cankered enemies in subjection and danger. And now,' said Sir Gawain, 'ye shall miss Sir Launcelot. But alas, I would not accord with him, and therefore,' said Sir Gawain, 'I pray you, fair uncle, that I may have paper, pen and ink, that I may write to Sir Launcelot a cedle with mine own hands.'

And then when paper and ink was brought, then Gawain was set up weakly by King Arthur, for he was shriven a little tofore; and then he wrote thus, as the French book maketh mention:

'Unto Sir Launcelot, flower of all noble knights that ever I heard of or saw by my days, I, Sir Gawain, King Lot's son of Orkney, sister's son unto the noble King Arthur, send thee greeting, and let thee have knowledge that the tenth day of May I was smitten upon the old wound that thou gavest me afore the city of Benwick, and through the same wound that thou gavest me I am come to my death day. And I will that all the world wit, that I, Sir Gawain, knight of the Table Round, sought my death, and not through thy deserving, but it was mine own seeking; wherefore I beseech thee, Sir Launcelot, to return again unto this realm, and see my tomb, and pray some prayer more or less for my soul. And this same day that I wrote this cedle, I was hurt to the death in the same wound, the which I had of thy hand, Sir Launcelot; for of a more nobler man might I not be slain.

'Also Sir Launcelot, for all the love that ever was betwixt us, make no tarrying, but come over the sea in all haste, that thou mayst with thy noble knights rescue that noble king that made thee knight, that is my lord Arthur, for he is full straitly bestad with a false traitor, that is my half-brother, Sir Mordred; and he hath let crown him king, and would have wedded my lady Queen Guenever, and so had he done had she not put herself in the Tower of London. And so the tenth day of May last past, my lord Arthur and we all landed upon them at Dover; and there we put that false traitor, Sir Mordred, to flight, and there it misfortuned me to be stricken upon thy stroke. And at the date of this letter was written, but two hours and an half afore my death, written with mine own hand, and so subscribed with part of my heart's blood. And I require thee, most famous knight of the world, that thou wilt see my tomb.'

And then Sir Gawain wept, and King Arthur wept; and then they swooned both. And when they awaked both, the king made Sir Gawain to receive his Saviour. And then Sir Gawain prayed the king for to send for Sir Launcelot, and to cherish him above all other knights.

And so at the hour of noon Sir Gawain yielded up the spirit; and then the king let inter him in a chapel within Dover Castle; and there yet all men may see the skull of him, and the same wound is seen that Sir Launcelot gave him in battle.

Then was it told the king that Sir Mordred had pitched a new field upon Barham Down. And upon the morn the king rode thither to him, and there was a great battle betwixt them, and much people was slain on both parties; but at the last Sir Arthur's party stood best, and Sir Mordred and his party fled unto Canterbury.

CHAPTER 3:

How after, Sir Gawain's ghost appeared to King Arthur, and warned him that he should not fight that day

And then the king let search all the towns for his knights that were slain, and interred them; and salved them with soft salves that so sore were wounded.

Then much people drew unto King Arthur. And then they said that Sir Mordred warred upon King Arthur with wrong. And then King Arthur drew him with his host down by the seaside westward toward Salisbury; and there was a day assigned betwixt King Arthur and Sir Mordred, that they should meet upon a down beside Salisbury, and not far from the seaside; and this day was assigned on a Monday after Trinity Sunday, whereof King Arthur was passing glad, that he might be avenged upon Sir Mordred.

Then Sir Mordred araised much people about London, for they of Kent, Sussex and Surrey, Essex, and of Suffolk, and of Norfolk, held the most part with Sir Mordred; and many a full noble knight drew unto Sir Mordred and to the king; but they loved Sir Launcelot drew unto Sir Mordred.

So upon Trinity Sunday at night, King Arthur dreamed a wonderful dream, and that was this: that him seemed he sat upon a chaflet in a chair, and the chair was fast to a wheel, and thereupon sat King Arthur in the richest cloth of gold that might be made; and the king thought there was under him, far from him, an hideous deep black water, and therein were all manner of serpents, and worms, and wild beasts, foul and horrible; and suddenly the king thought the wheel turned up-so-down, and he fell among the serpents, and every beast took him by a limb; and then the king cried as he lay in his bed and slept, 'Help.'

And then knights, squires, and yeomen, awaked the king; and then he was so amazed that he wist not where he was; and then he fell on slumbering again, not sleeping nor thoroughly waking.

So the king seemed verily that there came Sir Gawain unto him with a number of fair ladies with him. And when King Arthur saw him, then he said, 'Welcome my sister's son; I weened thou hadst been dead, and now I see thee alive, much am I beholding unto Almighty Jesu. O fair nephew and my sister's son, what be these ladies that hither be come with you?'

'Sir,' said Sir Gawain, 'all these be ladies for whom I have foughten when I was man living, and all these are those that I did battle for in righteous quarrel; and God hath given them that grace at their great prayer, because I did battle for them, that they should bring me hither unto you: thus much hath God given me leave, for to warn you of your death; for and ye fight as tomorn with Sir Mordred, as ye both have assigned, doubt ye not ye must be slain, and the most part of your people on both parties. And for the great grace and goodness that Almighty Jesu hath unto you, and for pity of you, and many more other good men there shall be slain, God hath sent me to you of his special grace, to give you warning that in no wise ye do battle as tomorn, but that ye take a treaty for a month day; and proffer you largely, so as tomorn to be put in a delay. For within a month shall come Sir Launcelot with all his noble knights, and rescue you worshipfully, and slay Sir Mordred, and all that ever will hold with him.'

Then Sir Gawain and all the ladies vanished. And anon the king called upon his knights, squires, and yeomen, and charged them wightly to fetch his noble lords and wise bishops unto him. And when they were come, the king told them his avision, what Sir Gawain had told him, and warned him that if he fought on the morn he should be slain.

Then the king commanded Sir Lucan the Butler, and his brother Sir Bedevere, with two bishops with them, and charged them in any wise, and they might: 'Take a treaty for a month day with Sir Mordred, and spare not, proffer him lands and goods as much as ye think best.'

So then they departed, and came to Sir Mordred, where he had a grim host of an hundred thousand men. And there they entreated Sir Mordred long time; and at the last Sir Mordred was agreed for to have Cornwall and Kent, by Arthur's days; after, all England, after the days of King Arthur.

CHAPTER 4:
How by misadventure of an adder the battle began, where Mordred was slain, and Arthur hurt to the death

Then were they condescended that King Arthur and Sir Mordred should meet betwixt both their hosts, and every each of them should bring fourteen persons; and they came with this word unto Arthur.

Then said he, 'I am glad that this is done': and so he went into the field.

And when Arthur should depart, he warned all his host that and they see any sword drawn, 'look ye come on fiercely, and slay that traitor, Sir Mordred, for I in no wise trust him.'

In likewise Sir Mordred warned his host that: 'And ye see any sword drawn, look that ye come on fiercely, and so slay all that ever before you standeth; for in no wise I will not trust for this treaty, for I know well my father will be avenged on me.'

And so they met as their pointment was, and so they were agreed and accorded thoroughly; and wine was fetched, and they drank.

Right soon came an adder out of a little heath bush, and it stung a knight on the foot. And when the knight felt him stungen, he looked down and saw the adder, and then he drew his sword to slay the adder, and thought of none other harm. And when the host on both parties saw that sword drawn, then they blew beams, trumpets, and horns, and shouted grimly. And so both hosts dressed them together.

And King Arthur took his horse, and said, 'Alas this unhappy day!' and so rode to his party. And Sir Mordred in likewise. And never was there seen a more dolefuller battle in no Christian land; for there was but rushing and riding, foining and striking, and many a grim word was there spoken either to other, and many a deadly stroke. But ever King Arthur rode throughout the battle of Sir Mordred many times, and did full nobly as a noble king should, and at all times he fainted never; and Sir Mordred that day put him in devoir, and in great peril. And thus they fought all the long day, and never stinted till the noble knights were laid to the cold earth; and ever they fought still till it was near night, and by that time was there an hundred thousand laid dead upon the down. Then was Arthur wood wroth out of measure, when he saw his people so slain from him.

Then the king looked about him, and then was he ware, of all his host and of all his good knights, were left no more alive but two knights; that one was Sir Lucan the Butler, and his brother Sir Bedevere, and they were full sore wounded.

'Jesu mercy,' said the king, 'where are all my noble knights becomen? Alas that ever I should see this doleful day, for now,' said Arthur, 'I am come to mine end. But would to God that I wist where were that traitor Sir Mordred, that hath caused all this mischief.'

Then was King Arthur ware where Sir Mordred leaned upon his sword among a great heap of dead men.

'Now give me my spear,' said Arthur unto Sir Lucan, 'for yonder I have espied the traitor that all this woe hath wrought.'

'Sir, let him be,' said Sir Lucan, 'for he is unhappy; and if ye pass this unhappy day ye shall be right well revenged upon him. Good lord, remember ye of your night's dream, and what the spirit of Sir Gawain told you this night, yet God of his great goodness hath preserved you hitherto. Therefore, for God's sake, my lord, leave off by this, for blessed be God ye have won the field, for here we be three alive, and with Sir Mordred is none alive; and if ye leave off now this wicked day of destiny is past.'

'Tide me death, betide me life,' saith the king, 'now I see him yonder alone he shall never escape mine hands, for at a better avail shall I never have him.'

'God speed you well,' said Sir Bedevere.

Then the king gat his spear in both his hands, and ran toward Sir Mordred, crying, 'Traitor, now is thy death day come.'

And when Sir Mordred heard Sir Arthur, he ran until

him with his sword drawn in his hand. And there King Arthur smote Sir Mordred under the shield, with a foin of his spear, throughout the body, more than a fathom. And when Sir Mordred felt that he had his death's wound he thrust himself with the might that he had up to the bur of King Arthur's spear. And right so he smote his father Arthur, with his sword holden in both his hands, on the side of the head, that the sword pierced the helmet and the brain pan, and therewithal Sir Mordred fell stark dead to the earth; and the noble Arthur fell in a swoon to the earth and there he swooned ofttimes.

And Sir Lucan the Butler and Sir Bedevere ofttimes heave him up. And so weakly they led him betwixt them both, to a little chapel not far from the seaside. And when the king was there he thought him well eased. Then heard they people cry in the field.

'Now go thou, Sir Lucan,' said the king, 'and do me to wit what betokens that noise in the field.'

So Sir Lucan departed, for he was grievously wounded in many places. And so as he yede, he saw and hearkened by the moonlight, how that pillers and robbers were comen into the field, to pill and to rob many a full noble knight of brooches, and beads, of many a good ring, and of many a rich jewel; and who that were not dead all out, there they slew them for their harness and their riches. When Sir Lucan understood this work, he came to the king as soon as he might, and told him all what he had heard and seen.

'Therefore by my rede,' said Sir Lucan, 'it is best that we bring you to some town.'

'I would it were so,' said the king.

CHAPTER 5:

How King Arthur commanded to cast his sword Excalibur into the water, and how he was delivered to ladies in a barge

'But I may not stand, mine head works so. Ah Sir Launcelot,' said King Arthur, 'this day have I sore missed thee: alas, that ever I was against thee, for now have I my death, whereof Sir Gawain me warned in my dream.'

Then Sir Lucan took up the king the one part, and Sir Bedevere the other part, and in the lifting the king swooned; and Sir Lucan fell in a swoon with the lift, that the part of his guts fell out of his body, and therewith the noble knight's heart brast. And when the king awoke, he beheld Sir Lucan, how he lay foaming at the mouth, and part of his guts lay at his feet.

'Alas,' said the king, 'this is to me a full heavy sight, to see this noble duke so die for my sake, for he would have holpen me, that had more need of help than I. Alas, he would not complain him, his heart was so set to help me: now Jesu have mercy upon his soul!'

Then Sir Bedevere wept for the death of his brother.

'Leave this mourning and weeping,' said the king, 'for all this will not avail me, for wit thou well and I might live myself, the death of Sir Lucan would grieve me evermore; but my time hieth fast,' said the king. 'Therefore,' said Arthur unto Sir Bedevere, 'take thou Excalibur, my good sword, and go with it to yonder water side, and when thou comest there I charge thee throw my sword in that water, and come again and tell me what thou there seest.'

'My lord,' said Bedevere, 'your commandment shall be done, and lightly bring you word again.'

So Sir Bedevere departed, and by the way he beheld that noble sword, that the pommel and the haft was all of precious stones; and then he said to himself, 'If I throw this rich sword in the water, thereof shall never come good, but harm and loss.' And then Sir Bedevere hid Excalibur under a tree.

And so, as soon as he might, he came again unto the king, and said he had been at the water, and had thrown the sword into the water.

'What saw thou there?' said the king.

'Sir,' he said, 'I saw nothing but waves and winds.'

'That is untruly said of thee', said the king, 'therefore go thou lightly again, and do my commandment; as thou art to me leve and dear, spare not, but throw it in.'

Then Sir Bedevere returned again, and took the sword in his hand; and then him thought sin and shame to throw away that noble sword, and so eft he hid the sword, and returned again, and told to the king that he had been at the water and done his commandment.

'What saw thou there?' said the king.

'Sir,' he said, 'I saw nothing but the waters wap and waves wan.'

'Ah, traitor untrue,' said King Arthur, 'now hast thou betrayed me twice. Who would have weened that thou that hast been to me so leve and dear, and thou art named a noble knight, and would betray me for the

riches of the sword? But now go again lightly, for thy
long tarrying putteth me in great jeopardy of my life, for
I have taken cold. And but if thou do now as I bid thee,
if ever I may see thee, I shall slay thee mine own hands;
for thou wouldst for my rich sword see me dead.'

Then Sir Bedevere departed, and went to the sword,
and lightly took it up, and went to the water side; and
there he bound the girdle about the hilts, and then he
threw the sword as far into the water as he might; and
there came an arm and an hand above the water and
met it, and caught it, and so shook it thrice and bran-
dished, and then vanished away the hand with the sword
in the water. So Sir Bedevere came again to the king,
and told him what he saw.

'Alas,' said the king, 'help me hence, for I dread me
I have tarried over long.'

Then Sir Bedevere took the king upon his back, and
so went with him to that water side. And when they
were at the water side, even fast by the bank hoved a
little barge with many fair ladies in it, and among them
all was a queen, and all they had black hoods, and all
they wept and shrieked when they saw King Arthur.

'Now put me into the barge,' said the king.

And so he did softly; and there received him three
queens with great mourning; and so they set them down,
and in one of their laps King Arthur laid his head.

And then that queen said, 'Ah, dear brother, why have
ye tarried so long from me? Alas, this wound on your
head hath caught over-much cold.'

And so then they rowed from the land, and Sir
Bedevere beheld all those ladies go from him.

Then Sir Bedevere cried, 'Ah my lord Arthur, what shall become of me, now ye go from me and leave me here alone among mine enemies?'

'Comfort thyself,' said the king, 'and do as well as thou mayest, for in me is no trust for to trust in; for I will into the vale of Avilion to heal me of my grievous wound: and if thou hear never more of me, pray for my soul.'

But ever the queens and ladies wept and shrieked, that it was pity to hear. And as soon as Sir Bedevere had lost the sight of the barge, he wept and wailed, and so took the forest; and so he went all that night, and in the morning he was ware betwixt two holts hoar, of a chapel and an hermitage.

CHAPTER 6:
How Sir Bedevere found him on the morn dead in an
hermitage, and how he abode there with the hermit

Then was Sir Bedevere glad, and thither he went; and when he came into the chapel, he saw where lay an hermit grovelling on all four, there fast by a tomb was new graven. When the hermit saw Sir Bedevere he knew him well, for he was but little tofore Bishop of Canterbury, that Sir Mordred flemed.

'Sir,' said Sir Bedevere, 'what man is there interred that ye pray so fast for?'

'Fair son,' said the hermit, 'I wot not verily, but by deeming. But this night, at midnight, here came a number of ladies, and brought hither a dead corpse, and prayed me to bury him; and here they offered an hundred tapers, and they gave me an hundred bezants.'

'Alas,' said Sir Bedevere, 'that was my lord King Arthur, that here lieth buried in this chapel.'

Then Sir Bedevere swooned; and when he awoke he prayed the hermit he might abide with him still there, to live with fasting and prayers. 'For from hence will I never go,' said Sir Bedevere, 'by my will, but all the days of my life here to pray for my lord Arthur.'

'Ye are welcome to me,' said the hermit, 'for I know you better than ye ween that I do. Ye are the bold Bedevere, and the full noble duke, Sir Lucan the Butler, was your brother.'

Then Sir Bedevere told the hermit all as ye have heard tofore. So there bode Sir Bedevere with the hermit that was tofore Bishop of Canterbury, and there Sir Bedevere put upon him poor clothes, and served the hermit full lowly in fasting and in prayers.

Thus of Arthur I find never more written in books that be authorised, nor more of the very certainty of his death heard I never read, but thus was he led away in a ship wherein were three queens; that one was King Arthur's sister, Queen Morgan le Fay; the other was the Queen of Northgales; the third was the Queen of the Waste Lands. Also there was Nimue, the chief lady of the lake, that had wedded Pelleas the good knight; and this lady had done much for King Arthur, for she would never suffer Sir Pelleas to be in no place where he should be in danger of his life; and so he lived to the uttermost of his days with her in great rest. More of the death of King Arthur could I never find, but that ladies brought him to his burials; and such one was buried there, that the hermit bare witness that sometime was Bishop of Canterbury, but yet the hermit knew not in certain that he was verily the body of King Arthur; for this tale Sir Bedevere, knight of the Table Round, made it to be written.

CHAPTER 7:

Of the opinion of some men of the death of King Arthur; and how Queen Guenever made her a nun in Almesbury

Yet some men say in many parts of England that King Arthur is not dead, but had by the will of Our Lord Jesu into another place; and men say that he shall come again, and he shall win the holy cross. I will not say that it shall be so, but rather I will say, here in this world he changed his life. But many men say that there is written upon his tomb this verse: HIC IACET ARTHURUS, REX QUONDAM REXQUE FUTURUS.

Thus leave I here Sir Bedevere with the hermit, that dwelled that time in a chapel beside Glastonbury, and there was his hermitage. And so they lived in their prayers, and fastings, and great abstinence.

And when Queen Guenever understood that King Arthur was slain, and all the noble knights, Sir Mordred and all the remnant, then the queen stole away, and five ladies with her, and so she went to Almesbury; and there she let make herself a nun, and ware white clothes and black, and great penance she took, as ever did sinful lady in this land, and never creature could make her merry; but lived in fasting, prayers, and alms-deeds, that all manner of people marvelled how virtuously she was changed.

Now leave we Queen Guenever in Almesbury, a nun in white clothes and black, and there she was abbess and ruler as reason would; and turn we from her, and speak we of Sir Launcelot du Lake.

CHAPTER 8:
How when Sir Launcelot heard of the death of King Arthur, and of Sir Gawain, and other matters, [he] came into England

And when he heard in his country that Sir Mordred was crowned king in England, and made war against King Arthur, his own father, and would let him to land in his own land, also it was told Sir Launcelot how that Sir Mordred had laid siege about the Tower of London, because the queen would not wed him, then was Sir Launcelot wroth out of measure, and said to his kinsmen,

'Alas, that double traitor Sir Mordred, now me repenteth that ever he escaped my hands, for much shame hath he done unto my lord Arthur; for all I feel by the doleful letter that my lord Sir Gawain sent me, on whose soul Jesu have mercy, that my lord Arthur is full hard bestad. Alas,' said Sir Launcelot, 'that ever I should live to hear that most noble king that made me knight thus to be overset with his subject in his own realm. And this doleful letter that my lord, Sir Gawain, hath sent me afore his death, praying me to see his tomb, wit you well his doleful words shall never go from mine heart, for he was a full noble knight as ever was born; and in an unhappy hour was I born that ever I should have that unhap to slay first Sir Gawain, Sir Gaheris the good knight, and mine own friend Sir Gareth, that full noble knight. Alas, I may say I am unhappy,' said Sir Launcelot, 'that ever I should do thus unhappily, and, alas, yet might I never have hap to slay that traitor, Sir Mordred.'

'Leave your complaints,' said Sir Bors, 'and first revenge you of the death of Sir Gawain; and it will be well done that ye see Sir Gawain's tomb, and secondly that ye revenge my lord Arthur, and my lady, Queen Guenever.'

'I thank you,' said Sir Launcelot, 'for ever ye will my worship.'

Then they made them ready in all the haste that might be, with ships and galleys, with Sir Launcelot and his host to pass into England. And so he passed over the sea till he came to Dover, and there he landed with seven kings, and the number was hideous to behold.

Then Sir Launcelot spered of men of Dover where was King Arthur become. Then the people told him how that he was slain, and Sir Mordred and an hundred thousand died on a day; and how Sir Mordred gave King Arthur there the first battle at his landing, and there was good Sir Gawain slain; and on the morn Sir Mordred fought with the king upon Barham Down, and there the king put Sir Mordred to the worse.

'Alas,' said Sir Launcelot, 'this is the heaviest tidings that ever came to me. Now, fair sirs,' said Sir Launcelot, 'show me the tomb of Sir Gawain.'

And then certain people of the town brought him into the Castle of Dover, and showed him the tomb. Then Sir Launcelot kneeled down and wept, and prayed heartily for his soul. And that night he made a dole, and all they that would come had as much flesh, fish, wine and ale, and every man and woman had twelve pence, come who would. Thus with his own hand dealt he this money, in a mourning gown; and ever he wept, and prayed them to pray for the soul of Sir Gawain. And on the morn all the priests and clerks that might be gotten in the country were there, and sang mass of requiem; and there offered first Sir Launcelot, and he offered an hundred pound; and then the seven kings offered forty pound apiece; and also there was a thousand knights, and each of them offered a pound; and the offering dured from morn till night, and Sir Launcelot lay two nights on his tomb in prayers and weeping. Then on the third day Sir Launcelot called the kings, dukes, earls, barons, and knights, and said thus:

'My fair lords, I thank you all of your coming into this country with me, but we came too late, and that shall repent me while I live, but against death may no man rebel. But sithen it is so,' said Sir Launcelot, 'I will myself ride and seek my lady, Queen Guenever, for as I hear say she hath had great pain and much disease; and I heard say that she is fled into the west. Therefore ye all shall abide me here, and but if I come again within fifteen days, then take your ships and your fellowship, and depart into your country, for I will do as I say to you.'

CHAPTER 9:
How Sir Launcelot departed to seek the queen Guenever, and how he found her at Almesbury

Then came Sir Bors de Ganis, and said, 'My lord Sir Launcelot, what think ye for to do, now to ride in this realm? Wit you well ye shall find few friends.'

'Be as be may,' said Sir Launcelot, 'keep you still here, for I will forth on my journey, and no man nor child shall go with me.'

So it was no boot to strive, but he departed and rode westerly, and there he sought a seven or eight days; and at the last he came to a nunnery, and then was Queen Guenever ware of Sir Launcelot as he walked in the cloister. And when she saw him there she swooned thrice, that all the ladies and gentlewomen had work enough to hold the queen up.

So when she might speak, she called ladies and gentlewomen to her, and said, 'Ye marvel, fair ladies, why I make this fare. Truly,' she said, 'it is for the sight of yonder knight that yonder standeth; wherefore I pray you all call him to me.'

When Sir Launcelot was brought to her, then she said to all the ladies, 'Through this man and me hath all this war been wrought, and the death of the most noblest knights of the world; for through our love that we have loved together is my most noble lord slain. Therefore, Sir Launcelot, wit thou well I am set in such a plight to get my soul health; and yet I trust through God's grace that after my death to have a sight of the blessed face of

Christ, and at doomsday to sit on His right side, for as sinful as ever I was are saints in heaven. Therefore, Sir Launcelot, I require thee and beseech thee heartily, for all the love that ever was betwixt us, that thou never see me more in the visage; and I command thee, on God's behalf, that thou forsake my company, and to thy kingdom thou turn again, and keep well thy realm from war and wrack; for as well as I have loved thee, mine heart will not serve me to see thee, for through thee and me is the flower of kings and knights destroyed; therefore, Sir Launcelot, go to thy realm, and there take thee a wife, and live with her with joy and bliss; and I pray thee heartily, pray for me to Our Lord that I may amend my misliving.'

'Now, sweet madam,' said Sir Launcelot, 'would ye that I should turn again unto my country, and there to wed a lady? Nay, madam, wit you well that shall I never do, for I shall never be so false to you of that I have promised; but the same destiny that ye have taken you to, I will take me unto, for to please Jesu, and ever for you I cast me specially to pray.'

'If thou wilt do so,' said the queen, 'hold thy promise, but I may never believe but that thou wilt turn to the world again.'

'Well, madam,' said he, 'ye say as pleaseth you, yet wist you me never false of my promise, and God defend but I should forsake the world as ye have done. For in the quest of the Sangrail I had forsaken the vanities of the world had not your lord been. And if I had done so at that time, with my heart, will, and thought, I had passed all the knights that were in the Sangrail except Sir Galahad, my son. And therefore, lady, sithen ye have taken you to perfection, I must needs take me to perfection, of right. For I take record of God, in you I have had mine earthly joy; and if I had founden you now so disposed, I had cast me to have had you into mine own realm.'

How Sir Launcelot came to the hermitage where the Archbishop of Canterbury was, and how he took the habit on him

'But sithen I find you thus disposed, I ensure you faithfully, I will ever take me to penance, and pray while my life lasteth, if that I may find any hermit, either gray or white, that will receive me. Wherefore, madam, I pray you kiss me and never no more.'

'Nay,' said the queen, 'that shall I never do, but abstain you from such works.' And they departed. But there was never so hard an hearted man but he would have wept to see the dolour that they made; for there was lamentation as they had been stungen with spears; and many times they swooned, and the ladies bare the queen to her chamber. And Sir Launcelot awoke, and went and took his horse, and rode all that day and all night in a forest, weeping.

And at the last he was ware of an hermitage and a chapel stood betwixt two cliffs; and then he heard a little bell ring to mass, and thither he rode and alit, and tied his horse to the gate, and heard mass. And he that sang mass was the Bishop of Canterbury.

Both the Bishop and Sir Bedevere knew Sir Launcelot, and they spake together after mass. But when Sir Bedevere had told his tale all whole, Sir Launcelot's heart almost brast for sorrow, and Sir Launcelot threw his arms abroad, and said, 'Alas, who may trust this world.'

And then he kneeled down on his knee, and prayed the Bishop to shrive him and assoil him. And then he besought the Bishop that he might be his brother.

Then the Bishop said, 'I will gladly,' and there he put an habit upon Sir Launcelot, and there he served God day and night with prayers and fastings.

Thus the great host abode at Dover. And then Sir Lionel took fifteen lords with him, and rode to London to seek Sir Launcelot; and there Sir Lionel was slain and many of his lords. Then Sir Bors de Ganis made the great host for to go home again; and Sir Bors, Sir Ector de Maris, Sir Blamor, Sir Bleoberis, with more other of Sir Launcelot's kin, took on them to ride all England overthwart and endlong, to seek Sir Launcelot. So Sir Bors by fortune rode so long till he came to the same chapel where Sir Launcelot was; and so Sir Bors heard a little bell knell, that rang to mass; and there he alit and heard mass. And when mass was done, the Bishop, Sir Launcelot, and Sir Bedevere, came to Sir Bors. And when Sir Bors saw Sir Launcelot in that manner clothing, then he prayed the Bishop that he might be in the same suit. And so there was an habit put upon him, and there he lived in prayers and fasting.

And within half a year, there was come Sir Galihud, Sir Galihodin, Sir Blamor, Sir Bleoberis, Sir Villiars, Sir Clarrus, and Sir Gahalantine. So all these seven noble knights there abode still. And when they saw Sir Launcelot had taken him to such perfection, they had no lust to depart, but took such an habit as he had. Thus they endured in great penance six year; and then Sir Launcelot took the habit of priesthood of the Bishop, and a twelvemonth he sang mass. And there was none of these other knights but they read in books, and holp for to sing mass, and rang bells, and did lowly all manner of service. And so their horses went where they would, for they took no regard of no worldly riches. For when they saw Sir Launcelot endure such penance, in prayers and fastings, they took no force what pain they endured, for to see the noblest knight of the world take such abstinence that he waxed full lean.

And thus upon a night, there came a vision to Sir Launcelot, and charged him, in remission of his sins, to haste him unto Almesbury: 'And by then thou come there, thou shalt find Queen Guenever dead. And therefore take thy fellows with thee, and purvey them of an horse bier, and fetch thou the corpse of her, and bury her by her husband, the noble King Arthur.' So this avision came to Sir Launcelot thrice in one night.

CHAPTER II:

How Sir Launcelot went with his seven fellows to Almesbury, and found there Queen Guenever dead, whom they brought to Glastonbury

Then Sir Launcelot rose up or day, and told the hermit.

'It were well done,' said the hermit, 'that ye made you ready, and that ye disobey not the avision.'

Then Sir Launcelot took his seven fellows with him, and on foot they yede from Glastonbury to Almesbury, the which is little more than thirty mile. And thither they came within two days, for they were weak and feeble to go. And when Sir Launcelot was come to Almesbury within the nunnery, Queen Guenever died but half an hour afore.

And the ladies told Sir Launcelot that Queen Guenever told them all or she passed, that Sir Launcelot had been priest near a twelvemonth, "And hither he cometh as fast as he may to fetch my corpse; and beside my lord, King Arthur, he shall bury me." Wherefore the queen said in hearing of them all, "I beseech Almighty God that I may never have power to see Sir Launcelot with my worldly eyen". 'And thus,' said all the ladies, 'was ever her prayer these two days, till she was dead.'

Then Sir Launcelot saw her visage, but he wept not greatly, but sighed. And so he did all the observance of the service himself, both the dirge, and on the morn he sang mass. And there was ordained an horse bier; and so with an hundred torches ever burning about the corpse of the queen, and ever Sir Launcelot with his seven fellows went about the horse bier, singing and reading many an holy orison, and frankincense upon the corpse incensed. Thus Sir Launcelot and his seven fellows went on foot from Almesbury unto Glastonbury.

And when they were come to the chapel and the hermitage, there she had a dirge, with great devotion. And on the morn the hermit that sometime was Bishop of Canterbury sang the mass of requiem with great devotion. And Sir Launcelot was the first that offered, and then all his eight fellows. And then she was wrapped in cered cloth of Rennes, from the top to the toe, in thirtyfold; and after she was put in a web of lead, and then in a coffin of marble. And when she was put in the earth Sir Launcelot swooned, and lay long still, while the hermit came and awaked him, and said, 'Ye be to blame, for ye displease God with such manner of sorrow making.'

'Truly,' said Sir Launcelot, 'I trust I do not displease God, for He knoweth mine intent. For my sorrow was not, nor is not, for any rejoicing of sin, but my sorrow may never have end. For when I remember of her beauty, and of her noblesse, that was both with her king and with her, so when I saw his corpse and her corpse so lie together, truly mine heart would not serve to sustain my careful body. Also when I remember me how by my default, and mine orgule and my pride, that they were both laid full low, that were peerless that ever was living of Christian people, wit you well,' said Sir Launcelot, 'this remembered, of their kindness and mine unkindness, sank so to mine heart, that I might not sustain myself.' So the French book maketh mention.

CHAPTER 12:

How Sir Launcelot began to sicken, and after died, whose body was borne to Joyous Gard for to be buried

Then Sir Launcelot never after ate but little meat, nor drank, till he was dead. For then he sickened more and more, and dried, and dwined away. For the Bishop nor none of his fellows might not make him to eat, and little he drank, that he was waxen by a cubit shorter than he was, that the people could not know him. For evermore, day and night, he prayed, but sometime he slumbered a broken sleep; ever he was lying grovelling on the tomb of King Arthur and Queen Guenever. And there was no comfort that the Bishop, nor Sir Bors, nor none of his fellows, could make him, it availed not.

So within six weeks after, Sir Launcelot fell sick, and lay in his bed; and then he sent for the Bishop that there was hermit, and all his true fellows. Then Sir Launcelot said with dreary steven, 'Sir Bishop, I pray you give to me all my rites that longeth to a Christian man.'

'It shall not need you,' said the hermit and all his fellows, 'it is but heaviness of your blood, ye shall be well mended by the grace of God tomorn.'

'My fair lords,' said Sir Launcelot, 'wit you well my careful body will into the earth, I have warning more than now I will say; therefore give me my rites.'

So when he was houselled and eneled, and had all that a Christian man ought to have, he prayed the Bishop that his fellows might bear his body to Joyous Gard.

Some men say it was Alnwick, and some men say it was Bamborough.

'Howbeit,' said Sir Launcelot, 'me repenteth sore, but I made mine avow sometime, that in Joyous Gard I would be buried. And because of breaking of mine avow, I pray you all, lead me thither.'

Then there was weeping and wringing of hands among his fellows. So at a season of the night they all went to their beds, for they all lay in one chamber. And so after midnight, against day, the Bishop that was hermit, as he lay in his bed asleep, he fell upon a great laughter. And therewithal the fellowship awoke, and come to the Bishop, and asked him what he ailed.

'Ah Jesu mercy,' said the Bishop, 'why did ye awake me? I was never in all my life so merry and so well at ease.'

'Wherefore?' said Sir Bors.

'Truly,' said the Bishop, 'here was Sir Launcelot with me with more angels than ever I saw men in one day. And I saw the angels heave up Sir Launcelot unto heaven, and the gates of heaven opened against him.'

'It is but dretching of swevens,' said Sir Bors, 'for I doubt not Sir Launcelot aileth nothing but good.'

'It may well be,' said the Bishop; 'go ye to his bed, and then shall ye prove the sooth.'

So when Sir Bors and his fellows came to his bed they found him stark dead, and he lay as he had smiled, and the sweetest savour about him that ever they felt. Then was there weeping and wringing of hands, and the greatest dole they made that ever made men.

And on the morn the Bishop did his mass of requiem;

and after, the Bishop and all the nine knights put Sir Launcelot in the same horse bier that Queen Guenever was laid in tofore that she was buried. And so the Bishop and they all together went with the body of Sir Launcelot daily, till they came to Joyous Gard; and ever they had an hundred torches burning about him. And so within fifteen days they came to Joyous Gard.

And there they laid his corpse in the body of the choir, and sang and read many psalters and prayers over him and about him. And ever his visage was laid open and naked, that all folks might behold him. For such was the custom in those days, that all men of worship should so lie with open visage till that they were buried.

And right thus as they were at their service, there came Sir Ector de Maris, that had seven year sought all England, Scotland, and Wales, seeking his brother, Sir Launcelot.

CHAPTER 13:
How Sir Ector found Sir Launcelot his brother dead, and how Constantine reigned next after Arthur; and of the end of this book

And when Sir Ector heard such noise and light in the choir of Joyous Gard, he alit and put his horse from him, and came into the choir, and there he saw men sing, weep, and all they knew Sir Ector, but he knew not them.

Then went Sir Bors unto Sir Ector, and told him how there lay his brother, Sir Launcelot, dead; and then Sir

Ector threw his shield, sword, and helm from him. And when he beheld Sir Launcelot's visage, he fell down in a swoon. And when he waked it were hard any tongue to tell the doleful complaints that he made for his brother.

'Ah Launcelot,' he said, 'thou were head of all Christian knights, and now I dare say,' said Sir Ector, 'thou Sir Launcelot, there thou liest, that thou were never matched of earthly knight's hand. And thou were the couteoust knight that ever bare shield. And thou were the truest friend to thy lover that ever bestrad horse. And thou were the truest lover of a sinful man that ever loved woman. And thou were the kindest man that ever struck with sword. And thou were the goodliest person that ever came among press of knights. And thou was the meekest man and the gentlest that ever ate in hall among ladies. And thou were the sternest knight to thy mortal foe that ever put spear in the rest.'

Then there was weeping and dolour out of measure. Thus they kept Sir Launcelot's corpse loft fifteen days, and then they buried it with great devotion.

And then at leisure they went all with the Bishop of Canterbury to his hermitage, and there they were together more than a month.

Then Sir Constantine, that was Sir Cador's son of Cornwall, was chosen king of England. And he was a full noble knight, and worshipfully he ruled this realm. And then this King Constantine sent for the Bishop of Canterbury, for he heard say where he was. And so he was restored unto his bishopric, and left that hermitage. And Sir Bedevere was there ever still hermit to his life's end.

Then Sir Bors de Ganis, Sir Ector de Maris, Sir Gahalantine, Sir Galihud, Sir Galihodin, Sir Blamore, Sir Bleoberis, Sir Villiars le Valiant, Sir Clarrus of Cleremont, all these knights drew them to their countries. Howbeit King Constantine would have had them with him, but they would not abide in this realm. And there they all lived in their countries as holy men.

And some English books maken mention that they went never out of England after the death of Sir Launcelot, but that was but favour of makers. For the French book maketh mention, and is authorised, that Sir Bors, Sir Ector, Sir Blamor, and Sir Bleoberis, went into the Holy Land thereas Jesu Christ was quick and dead, and anon as they had stablished their lands. For the book saith, so Sir Launcelot commanded them for to do, or ever he passed out of this world. And these four knights did many battles upon the miscreants or Turks. And there they died upon a Good Friday for God's sake.